The Cupcake Diaries: Taste of Romance

Also by Darlene Panzera

The Cupcake Diaries: Recipe for Love
The Cupcake Diaries: Sweet On You
Bet You'll Marry Me

THE CUPCAKE DIARIES
Taste of
Romance

DARLENE PANZERA

AVONIMPULSE
An Imprint of HarperCollinsPublishers

Excerpt from *The Cupcake Diaries: Sweet On You* copyright © 2013 by Darlene Panzera.

Excerpt from *The Cupcake Diaries: Recipe for Love* copyright © 2013 by Darlene Panzera.

Excerpt from *Stealing Home* copyright © 2013 by Candice Wakoff.

Excerpt from *Lucky Like Us* copyright © 2013 by Jennifer Ryan.

Excerpt from *Stuck On You* copyright © 2013 by Cheryl Harper.

Excerpt from *The Right Bride* copyright © 2013 by Jennifer Ryan.

Excerpt from *Lachlan's Bride* copyright © 2013 by Kathleen Harrington.

EPub Edition JUNE 2013 ISBN: 9780062242839

Print Edition ISBN: 9780062242853

JV 10 9 8 7 6 5 4 3 2 1

For my children,
Samantha, Robert, and Jason

Chapter One

All I really need is love, but a little chocolate now and then doesn't hurt!

—Charles Schulz

FOCUS, KIM REPRIMANDED herself. *Keep to the task at hand and stop eavesdropping on other people's conversations.*

But she didn't need to hear the crack of the teenage boy's heart to feel his pain. Or to remember the last time she'd heard the wretched words "I'm leaving" spoken to her.

She tried to ignore the couple as she picked up the pastry bag filled with pink icing and continued to decorate the tops of the strawberry preserve cupcakes. However, the discussion between the high school boy and what she assumed to be his girlfriend kept her attentive.

"When will I see you again?" he asked.

Kim glanced toward them and leaned closer.

"I don't know," the girl replied.

The soft lilt in her accent thrust the familiarity of the conversation even deeper into Kim's soul.

"I'll be going to the university for two years," the girl continued. "Maybe we meet again after."

Not likely. Kim shook her head, and her stomach tightened. From past experience, she knew once the school year was over in June, most foreign students went home, never to return.

And left many broken hearts in their wake.

"Two years is a long time," the boy said.

Forever was even longer. Kim drew in a deep breath as the unmistakable catch in the poor boy's voice replayed again and again in her mind. And her heart.

How long were they going to stand there and torment her by reminding her of her parting four years earlier with Gavin, the Irish student she'd dated through college? Dropping the bag of icing on the Creative Cupcakes counter, she moved toward them.

"Can I help you?" Kim asked, pulling on a new pair of food handler's gloves.

"I'll have the white chocolate macadamia," the girl said, pointing to the cupcake she wanted in the glass display case.

The boy dug his hands into his pockets, counted the meager change he'd managed to withdraw, and turned five shades of red.

"None for me." His Adam's apple bobbed as he swallowed. "How much for hers?"

"You have to have one, too," the girl protested. "It's your birthday."

Kim took one look at his lost-for-words expression and said, "If today is your birthday, the cupcakes are free." She added, "For both you and your guest."

The teenager's face brightened. "Really?"

Kim nodded and removed the cupcakes the two love-birds wanted from the display case. She even put a birthday candle on one of them, a heart on the other. Maybe the girl would come back for him. Or he would fly to Ireland for her. *Maybe.*

Her eyes stung, and she squeezed them shut for a brief second. When she opened them again, she set her jaw. Enough was enough. Now that they had their cupcakes, she could escape back into her work and forget about romance and relationships and every regrettable moment she'd ever wasted on love.

She didn't need it. Not like her older sister, Andi, who had recently lost her heart to Jake Hartman, their Creative Cupcakes financier and reporter for the *Astoria Sun*. Or like her other co-owner friend, Rachel, who had just gotten engaged to Mike Palmer, a miniature model maker for movies who also doubled as the driver of their Cupcake Mobile.

All she needed was to dive deep into her desire to put paint on canvas. She glanced at the walls of the cupcake shop, adorned with her scenic oil, acrylic, and watercolor paintings. Maybe if she worked hard enough, she'd have the money to open her own art gallery, and she wouldn't need to decorate cupcakes anymore.

But for now, she needed to serve the next customer. *Where was Rachel?*

"Hi, Kim." Officer Ian Lockwell, one of their biggest supporters, sat on one of the stools lining the marble cupcake counter. "I'm wondering if you have the back party room available on June twenty-seventh?"

Kim reached under the counter and pulled out the three-ring binder she, Andi, and Rachel had dubbed the Cupcake Diary to keep track of all things cupcake related. Looking at the calendar, she said, "Yes, the date is open. What's the occasion?"

"My wife and I have been married almost fifteen years," the big, square-jawed cop told her. "We're planning on renewing our vows on our anniversary and need a place to celebrate with friends and family."

"No better place to celebrate love than Creative Cupcakes," Kim assured him, glancing around at all the couples in the shop. "I'll put you on the schedule."

Next, the door opened, and a stream of romance writers filed in for their weekly meeting. Kim pressed her lips together. The group intimidated her with their watchful eyes and poised pens. They scribbled in their notebooks whenever she walked by as if writing down her every move, and she didn't want to give them any useful fodder. She hoped Rachel could take their orders, if she could find her.

"Rachel?"

No answer, but the phone rang—a welcome distraction. She picked up and said, "Creative Cupcakes, this is Kim."

"What are you doing there? I thought you were going to take time off."

Kim pushed into the privacy of the kitchen, glad it was Andi and not another customer despite the impending lecture tone. "I still have several dozen cupcakes to decorate."

"Isn't Rachel there with you?"

The door of the walk-in pantry burst open, and Rachel and Mike emerged, wrapped in each other's arms, laughing and grinning.

Kim rolled her eyes. "Yes, Rachel's here."

Rachel extracted herself from Mike's embrace and mouthed the word "sorry."

But Kim knew she wasn't. Rachel had been in her own red-headed, happy bubble ever since macho, dark-haired Mike the Magnificent had proposed two weeks earlier.

"I'll be in for my shift as soon as I get Mia off to afternoon kindergarten," Andi continued, "and the shop's way ahead in sales. There's no reason you can't take a break. Ever since you broke up with Gavin, you've become a workaholic."

Kim sucked in her breath at the mention of his name. Only Andi dared to ever bring him up.

"Gavin has nothing to do with my work."

"You never date."

"I'm concentrating on my career."

"It's been years since you've been out with anyone. You need to slow down, take time to smell the roses."

"Smell the roses?" Kim gasped. "Are you *serious?*"

"Go on an adventure," Andi amended.

"Working is an adventure."

"You used to dream of a different kind of adventure," Andi said, lowering her voice. "The kind that requires a passport."

Kim wished she'd never picked up the phone. Just because her sister had her life put back together didn't mean she had the right to tell her how to live.

"Painting cupcakes and canvas is the only adventure I need right now. I promised Dad I'd have the money to pay him for my new art easel by the end of the week."

"Dad doesn't care about the money, but he does care about you. He asked me to call."

"He did?" Kim stopped in front of the sink and rubbed her temples with her fingertips. Her sister was known to overreact, but their father? He didn't voice concern unless it was legitimate.

With the phone to her ear, she returned to the front counter of the couple-filled cupcake shop, her heart screaming louder and louder with each consecutive beat.

They were *everywhere.* By the window, at the tables, next to the display case. Couples, couples, couples. Everyone had a partner, had someone.

Almost everyone.

Instead of Goonies Day, the celebration of the 1985 release date of *The Goonies* movie, which was filmed in Astoria, she would have thought the calendar had been flipped back to Valentine's Day at Creative Cupcakes. And in her opinion, one Valentine's Day a year was more than enough.

She reached a hand into the pocket of her pink apron and clenched the golden wings she had received on her first airplane flight as a child. The pin never left her side, and like the flying squirrel tattooed on her shoulder, it reminded her of her dream to fly, if not to another land, then at least to the farthest reaches of her imagination.

Where her heart would be free.

Okay, maybe she *did* spend too much time at the cupcake shop. "Tell Dad not to worry," Kim said into the phone. "Tell him . . . I'm taking the afternoon off."

"Promise?" Andi persisted.

Oh, yeah. Tearing off her apron, she turned around and threw it over Rachel's and Mike's heads. "I'm heading out the door now."

FIVE MINUTES LATER, Kim stood outside the cupcake shop on Marine Drive, wondering which direction to go. The tattoo parlor was on her left, a boutique to her right, and the waterfront walk beneath the giant arching framework of the Astoria–Megler Bridge stretched straight in front.

Turning her back on it all, she decided to take a new path and soon discovered an open wrought iron gate along Bond Road. This had to be the side entrance to Astoria's new community park, the one Andi had been raving about the week before, and hadn't her sister told her to "smell the roses"?

Kim walked through the gate toward a large circle of white rosebushes and began to count off each flower as she leaned in to fill her lungs with their strong, fragrant scent. "One, two, three . . ."

After smelling seventeen, she moved toward the yellows. "Eighteen, nineteen, twenty . . ."

Past the gazebo she found red roses, orange roses, and a vast variety of purples and pinks. "Forty-six, forty-seven, forty-eight . . ."

Her artist's eye took in the palette of color, and imagining the scene on canvas, she wished she'd brought along her paints and brushes. "Sixty-two, sixty-three, sixty-four . . ."

Andi had been right. The sweet, perfumed scent of the roses did seem to ease her tension and help block out all thoughts of romance. Even if the rose was a notorious symbol of *love*. And the flower that garnished the most sales over *romantic* holidays. With petals used for flower girl baskets at *weddings*.

Who needed romance anyway? Not her.

She bent to smell the next group of flowers and noticed a tall, blond man with work gloves carrying a potted rosebush past the ivy trellis. As his gaze caught hers, he appeared to pause. Then he smiled.

Kim smiled back and moved toward the next rose.

"Can I help you?" the gardener asked, walking over.

Oh, *no*. He had a foreign accent, Scandinavian, like some of the locals whose ancestors first inhabited the area. And she had an acute weakness for foreign accents.

"I think I need to do this myself," Kim replied. "My goal is to smell a hundred roses."

"Why a hundred?"

"That's the number of things on my to-do list. I thought stopping to smell one rose per task might balance out my life."

"Interesting concept." The attractive gardener appeared to suppress a grin. "How many more do you have to go?"

"I'm at sixty-seven."

"I didn't mean to interrupt." He set the rosebush down, took off a glove, and extended his hand. "I'm Nathaniel Sjölander."

"Kimberly Burke," she said, accepting the handshake. His hand, much larger than her own, surrounded hers with warmth.

"I have to load a couple dozen roses into my truck for the Portland Rose Festival tomorrow, but by all means—keep sniffing."

Kim pulled rose number sixty-eight toward her, a yellow flower as buttery and delicately layered as a . . . freshly baked croissant. Hunger sprang to life inside her empty stomach, and she realized she'd been so busy working, she'd forgotten to eat lunch.

She watched Nathaniel Sjölander move between the potted plants. Was he single? Would someone like him be interested in her? Maybe ask her to dinner? And why *hadn't* she dated anyone in the past few years? She could argue that good-looking single men were hard to come by, but the truth was, she just hadn't taken the initiative to find one.

Nathaniel made several trips back and forth between the greenhouse and the gate, his gaze sliding toward her again and again. *Oh, yes!* He was definitely interested. Her pulse quickened as he approached her a second time.

"I think you missed a few." Nathaniel pulled a cut bouquet of red roses from behind his back and presented them to her.

"Thank you." She hugged the flowers against her chest and lifted her gaze from the Sjölander's Garden Nursery business logo embroidered on his tan work shirt to his warm, kind . . . *blue* eyes.

Oh, man, why did they have to be *blue*? Blue was her favorite color. She could get lost in blue. Especially *his* blue, a blend of sparkling azure with a hint of sea green. Reminded her of the ripples in the water where the Columbia River met the Pacific Ocean just a few miles outside Astoria.

"Sjölander. Is that Finnish?" she asked.

"Swedish. Most of my family resides in Sweden, with the exception of my brother and a few cousins."

His name was incredibly familiar. Where had she come across the name Sjölander before? The Cupcake Diary!

"I'm co-owner of Creative Cupcakes," Kim informed him. "Didn't you book us for an upcoming event?"

"Must be for the wedding."

Wedding? She held her breath. "*Yours?*"

He flashed her a smile. "No. My brother's."

"Of course." She breathed easy once again.

"They've decided to have the ceremony in the new community park."

Kim looked around, confused. "Isn't *this* the new community park?"

Nathaniel laughed. "The park is two blocks down the street and much larger than my backyard."

"Your *backyard*?"

Kim's mouth popped open in an embarrassed *O*. Heat seared her cheeks. No wonder he'd been watching her. He was probably wondering what crazy chick was wandering around his property!

And as for the flowers? She doubted he meant them to symbolize anything romantic. Why would he? She was an idiot! The guy was probably just trying to be nice. Or maybe he thought giving her flowers would encourage her to leave. Worse—she would have to face him again in a few weeks at his brother's wedding.

With an inward groan she squeezed her eyes shut, wishing she could start the day over. Or maybe the whole last decade. Then without further ado she set her jaw and looked up.

"Thanks for the roses," she mumbled. And before she could embarrass herself further, she hurried out the gate and back to the cupcake shop—where she belonged.

Chapter Two

One who plants a garden plants happiness.

—Chinese proverb

KIM WALKED INTO the Creative Cupcakes kitchen, found a vase for her bouquet, and set up her art easel in the back corner of the shop. Andi barely noticed her. She stood at the front counter admiring Rachel's engagement ring.

Both women had been acting like silly, love-struck sixteen-year-olds since they'd found "their man." Kim prided herself on keeping her emotions tucked away. She wouldn't lose her head or make a public spectacle of herself. If a guy liked her, he could ask her out. If she liked him, she'd say yes. There was no need to get all silly about it.

Dipping her brush into the paint jar of crimson blush, she swept the images of Nathaniel's garden from her mind and on to the white canvas board in front of her. Next, she used a lighter shade, also one of the names of their cupcakes, pink champagne.

Lewy, Rachel's grandfather, sat at the table beside her easel and raised a finger toward her art. "If I could fit that into my memory box, I'd take it home with me."

Kim glanced at the old man, who had Alzheimer's, and the large cardboard shoebox in front of him. He carried the box filled with personal mementos with him wherever he went. Rachel and her mother had pasted family photographs on the top and sides to help him remember whenever his mind got stuck.

Rachel stepped up beside them. "You like Kim's painting, Grandpa?"

He nodded. "She paints love on canvas."

Kim hesitated, glanced at him, then her work, and frowned. All she saw were roses.

Before she could respond, Andi joined them. "Creative Cupcakes is doing so well with sales, we'll finally have some extra money to spend. I haven't bought myself new clothes in years, and I can't wait to get a new wardrobe for my trip to Hawaii with Jake."

"You scored big when Danielle offered you the trip tickets she won from the Crab, Seafood, and Wine Festival," Rachel said, then burst into a big smile the way she always did when thinking about her fiancé. "As for me, I'm saving for my wedding. Mike and I decided to get married on Christmas Eve."

Andi gasped. "You set a date?"

"Yes!" Rachel's eyes sparkled. "And I'd like both of you to be my bridesmaids."

"I'd love to," Grandpa Lewy agreed.

Kim placed another dab of pink on the tip of one of her painted roses and laughed. "I think Rachel meant Andi and me."

"Of course I'll be your bridesmaid," Andi said, wrapping her arms around her best friend.

"Me, too," Kim added.

"Grandpa, since Daddy's gone, you can walk me down the aisle," Rachel told him.

Grandpa Lewy grinned. "I walked down the aisle once. Beautiful day that was. I'd love to walk down the aisle again."

Andi's face took on a dreamy, far-off expression. "I'll be able to buy new clothes for my trip, Rachel will be able to have an absolutely gorgeous wedding—with all the fanciest trimmings."

"Of course!" Rachel agreed.

"And I bet Kim wants some new paints and canvases, right, Kim?" Andi asked.

Kim hesitated. She wanted a whole lot more than art supplies. Since her paintings won first place in the Portland show the week before, she'd been offered the chance to open her own art gallery with a few of the other artists. But if she accepted, she feared she wouldn't have time for the cupcake shop, a fact she was reluctant to tell them.

"New paint and canvas," Kim repeated and managed a weak smile. "Yeah, something like that."

A loud, tinkering clatter sounded from outside, and Kim turned her head toward the large front window in time to see the 1933 bread loaf–shaped antique Cupcake Mobile pull up to the curb. It was Mike returning from his latest delivery. He got out of the truck, and walked toward the shop. He nodded at an older man who was walking toward the shop, too—Sam Warden, the owner of their building.

"He's here!" Andi exclaimed.

Rachel kept her eyes on Mike as he whisked through the front door, followed by their landlord. "Yes, he is."

"I meant Mr. Warden," Andi corrected. "Today we sign the new lease."

Kim's mouth fell open. How could she have forgotten? She should have told Andi about her possible future plans. Now their three-month trial lease agreement was up, and they'd sign another lease lasting a whole year. Could she work at an art gallery and Creative Cupcakes, too?

Mr. Warden greeted them but avoided their gaze. Kim put down her brush and watched him glance nervously about the shop at all the customers. Something wasn't right.

"Where's Jake Hartman?" he asked.

"He'll be here soon," Andi promised. "He knows what an important day this is. We're all very excited."

Everyone except the building owner, Kim mused and got up to follow them to the front counter.

"Where is it?" Andi asked. "Can I see the new lease?"

Mr. Warden shook his head and finally looked her straight in the eye. "I'm sorry."

Rachel and Mike exchanged a quick glance, and doubt crossed Andi's face as she caught on to the landlord's apprehensive mood.

"What do you mean, 'I'm sorry'?" Andi said, her voice dropping.

"I have to sell the building," he told them.

Andi stiffened. Rachel pursed her lips, and Mike put a hand on her arm, as if to offer support.

Kim glanced at each of them, then up to the long golden cake knife on the wall, the symbol of their shop's success when they first opened.

"What does this mean for us?" Andi demanded.

Mr. Warden wiped his brow with one hand. "I'll give you a temporary lease to continue the shop until somebody buys the building, but then you either have to close down or move to a different location. Unless you buy the building yourself."

"We can't close," Andi protested. "Not after all the hard work we've put into this place over the past few months."

"And there aren't any other places available with a prime location like we have here," Rachel said, waving one of her perfectly manicured hands.

Kim bit her lower lip. If Creative Cupcakes closed, she wouldn't feel guilty about telling Andi and Rachel she wanted to leave to open her own gallery. On the other hand, she'd discovered she had other artistic talents while working at the shop, like cupcake decorating, and she, Andi, and Rachel had had a lot of fun together. She wasn't sure she could let it all go.

"Can we afford to buy the building?" she asked.

Their stooped, gray-haired landlord told them the price, and an unexpected stream of sadness seeped through her memories and left her hollow.

Andi ran her hands down her apron. "Will you take payments?"

Mr. Warden shook his head. "I would if I could, but my son is very ill. My wife and I have to move to Georgia to be with him and pay his medical costs."

Leaving the temporary lease papers on the counter for them to sign, he attempted a hasty exit and almost ran over the mail carrier on his way out.

For several moments they were all silent. Even the chatter from the customers sitting at the white round tables eating their cupcakes seemed to turn into whispers.

Then Andi raised her chin and her face took on that steely look of resolve Kim had seen so many times while growing up.

"The shop has had great sales, and we can work hard this month to gain even more," Andi declared. "We can do this."

"Buy the building," Rachel repeated. She didn't look as confident as Andi but shrugged and gave them each a mischievous grin. "Hey, why not?"

"It's a lot of money," Kim warned. "We got turned down for a loan when we first opened, and I'm not sure three months of sales stats will be enough to change anyone's mind."

Andi reached under the counter and pulled out the Cupcake Diary and a pen. "Do you remember what

Mom used to say whenever we said something was too hard?"

Kim nodded. "'Faith can move mountains.'"

"So we have a mountain to move."

"We'll need to set up a stand at more fairs and festivals," Rachel said, pointing to the calendar. "Book more outside events. I can initiate a promo blitz across the Internet."

"First we need to hire help." Andi scribbled a note in the cookbook-style diary. "I've had to turn away at least a dozen catering opportunities over the past two weeks because we couldn't produce enough cupcakes."

Kim agreed. Hiring other employees was a *great* idea. If she left, one of them could take her place.

"I'll give you money if you give me a cupcake," Grandpa Lewy said, his memory box under one arm as he made his way over to the display case.

"No, Grandpa," Rachel told him. "You've already had one."

"I don't remember having one," he argued.

Rachel laughed. "I think you do. You never forget about cupcakes."

"That's because they're so good," he replied.

"We could sell cupcakes at the Scandinavian Festival," Kim suggested. "And maybe host a Father's Day event. 'Cupcakes with Dad.' All the kids can bring their fathers into the shop, and they can eat cupcakes together."

Andi shot her a wistful look. "Do you think *our* dad would come into the shop?"

Kim held her gaze, not knowing the answer. Their

father hadn't been there often for them in the past. Not since their mother had died.

"I'll be your dad," Rachel's grandfather offered. "I'll eat a cupcake with you."

"Of course you would," Andi said, squeezing his shoulder. "I also think we should sell our mixes online, make Creative Cupcakes a household name, and ship them all over the U.S."

Kim couldn't bear to see her sister's perseverance and hard-fought dream to run a cupcake shop crushed.

"Why stop there?" she added. "Why don't we ship worldwide?"

"You're right!" Andi exclaimed. "Creative Cupcakes, worldwide distributor!"

Guy Armstrong, the white-ponytailed tattoo artist from next door, walked in and grinned. "You can distribute some cupcakes my way. I'm here to pick up my order."

"I put it right—" Rachel frowned. "I thought I put it on the end of the counter. Let me go check the kitchen."

As Rachel disappeared through the kitchen's double doors, Guy's face lit up, and he rubbed his hands together. "What are we brainstorming this time? How to defeat desperate cupcake-hating housewives? Or how to bring Creative Cupcakes to national TV?"

"We need to buy the building," Andi told him. "Then we'll have the golden cupcake cutter, our trophy from the cupcake war, *and* the keys to success."

"Did I hear the word 'success'?" Jake asked, smiling as he came through the door with an armful of yellow roses.

"Oh, Jake, I'm so glad you're here," Andi said, a catch in her voice.

"Sorry I'm late," he said, drawing close to her side. "I stopped to pick up these from Sjölander's Garden Nursery."

"Sjölander's?" Kim glanced from the yellow roses Jake held to the red roses she'd put in the vase by her easel.

If she'd met the blond-haired, blue-eyed Swede in his garden shop instead of stumbling into his backyard, he might have thought better of her, maybe even asked her out on a date.

Not that she *needed* a date. She was perfectly happy without one. One hundred percent happy.

Andi took the flowers in her arms. "They're beautiful. But, Jake, did you hear? We didn't get the new lease."

Jake's eyes widened, and a crease formed on his brow. "We didn't?"

Andi informed him of the landlord's predicament and laid out their options. "Do you have any ideas?"

"I did have one idea when I arrived," Jake said and got down on one knee.

"I couldn't find your order, Guy," Rachel announced, coming back into the front room. "But I boxed up a fresh—*Oh my gosh!* Jake, are you—*Oh!* I'm so sorry to interrupt—go ahead!"

Jake grinned up at Andi's startled face. "Andrea Leanne Burke, no matter what happens in this whole wide world, I promise to love you. I don't have all the answers, but I do have a question. Will you marry me?"

Kim gasped. Or maybe it was Andi. Or maybe even

Guy. For a moment it seemed as if something had sucked the air out of the entire room.

Then Jake held up a coconut macaroon cupcake with a glistening diamond ring sticking up out of the center.

"Yes!" Andi broke into a huge smile. "Oh, Jake, I love you so much."

"And you already have tickets to Hawaii for your honeymoon," Rachel reminded them.

"I'd get married in Hawaii, but Kim's afraid to fly," Andi confessed. "And I can't get married without my sister there. Oh, Jake, I can't wait to tell the girls. Now Mia and Taylor will be sisters, too. And if we marry and move in together, we'll save money on rent."

"That's not why I proposed," Jake teased, standing up.

"I know," Andi said, "but it will still help us save money to buy the shop."

Kim froze, her stomach turning as fast as her thoughts. If Jake and his daughter, Taylor, moved into the small house with Andi and Mia, there would be no room for her. She couldn't move back in with her father. His new house in Warrenton didn't have enough space for her either. She'd need to use the money she won from the recent art show to rent her own apartment, not open a gallery with her friends.

And if Creative Cupcakes closed, how would she continue to pay rent? Instead of choosing between jobs, she wouldn't have any job at all.

Handsome, brown-haired, brown-eyed Jake, dressed like a modern-day prince in his tan three-piece suit, kissed her sister and swooped her up into his arms.

"What if I told you I've wanted to propose since the night you first came up to me in the Captain's Port and tried to buy my cupcake?"

Andi brushed a long strand of her dark blond hair behind her ear. "What if I told you I've dreamed of marrying you since the moment you shared it with me?"

Andi and Jake kissed again, and Rachel jumped up and down, squealing with delight. Her grandfather chuckled and hugged his memory box. Guy and the customers at the surrounding tables whistled and clapped.

Kim clapped, too, and gave a start when she realized tears were running down her face. Happy tears. Of course they were happy. What other kind of tears would they be?

Her big sis deserved to be happy. Andi had been through a tough time trying to support her six-year-old daughter without any help from her deadbeat ex. And Jake, whose wife had died and left him with a kindergartner of his own, was perfect for her. Absolutely perfect.

Kim brushed another tear off her cheek, and Guy nudged her with his elbow. "Looks like we're the Last of the Mohicans."

"The last what?" she asked.

"The last of the 'single' tribe."

"I guess so," Kim agreed, not sure she liked the forlorn way he said it.

She watched Jake slide the ring on Andi's finger, and her chest tightened. *How she wished it were her!* How she wished she could find a great, handsome prince and live happily ever after like Rachel and Andi.

Maybe she'd watched too many Disney movies with

her niece. But that's what made the movies so special. Happily-ever-afters didn't come to everyone. They were as rare as a full sun in an Oregon winter.

Thank goodness no one knew what was really going on inside her at this moment, because it wasn't pretty. And it wasn't right for her to feel jealous or left out.

It was her own fault she was single. She'd had the chance to make her relationship with Gavin work. She could have said yes when he asked her to fly off to Europe with him at the end of their last college semester. But she couldn't. Her fear of flying had made it impossible for her to say anything but no.

"Kim, can you believe it?" Andi asked, holding out her hand. The hand with the ring, of course.

Kim forced her legs to walk forward, forced her arms to wrap themselves around Andi and give her a hug. Then, smiling past the hurt, she said the words she knew her sister longed to hear.

"I am so happy for you."

Chapter Three

There is only one happiness in life: to love and
be loved.

—George Sand

MONDAY MORNING KIM, Andi, and Rachel gathered
around one of Creative Cupcakes' round dining tables.
Mia and Taylor joined them. Both six-year-olds were in
the same afternoon kindergarten class and spent their
mornings at the shop determined to lend a hand. Or two.

Kim slid into a chair and took a new three-ring binder
out of her paisley print hobo bag. "Time for a new Cupcake Diary."

"Why are there keys?" Mia asked, pointing to the
cover.

"Because," Kim said, scooping her niece up into her

lap, "we need Mr. Warden to let us keep the keys to this building."

"The keys can represent 'the keys to success,'" Rachel added. "I like it."

"My turn," Taylor insisted, as if playing a game. "Why do the keys have wings?"

Andi shrugged. "Because the keys will fly away if we don't make enough money?"

Kim nodded. "With our dreams."

Taking out a pen, she opened and wrote in the new diary:

Goal #1: Buy the building.

"What's that?" Mia asked, pulling a booklet out from under the diary.

Kim looked above Mia's head to meet her mother's gaze. "The listings for apartment rentals."

"You don't have to find one right away," Andi said in a rush. "Jake and Taylor won't be moving in until the wedding. You know I'd never kick you out."

"That's good," Kim assured her. "Because I don't think I can rent an apartment until I'm positive I'm going to have a job at the end of the month."

"I know what you mean," Rachel said, bobbing her red curls. "How can I plan my wedding until I know if we can keep Creative Cupcakes? I won't know how much money I'll have available."

The door opened, and a delivery man in a brown uniform brought in a large bouquet of red roses.

Andi smiled as she got up and met him halfway. "I bet they're from Jake!"

"You think Jake's the only guy who sends flowers?" Rachel teased, scooting her chair back and hurrying to her side. "They could be from Mike for *me*. Especially since they're red, and Jake knows you like yellow."

"They're from Sjölander's," Andi insisted, "the same place Jake got the other ones."

"Don't you think other people buy roses from Sjölander's?" Rachel asked, reaching for the tag.

Kim glanced at the two little girls left at the table with her. "What do *you* think?"

Mia laughed. "I think they're for me."

"Or me," Taylor agreed.

"They're for Kim."

The note of surprise in her sister's voice made Kim look up, and the expression on Andi's face held a host of unspoken questions.

Rachel smiled and read, "'Dear Kim, why stop at one hundred? Sincerely, Nathaniel.'"

Kim shot out of her chair and took a look at the tag.

"Who's Nathaniel?" Andi asked.

"And what does he mean, 'why stop at one hundred'?" Rachel added.

Kim took the roses in her arms and drew in a whiff of their deep scent. "I met Nathaniel Sjölander at . . . the new park, or what I thought was the new park."

"And?" Andi prompted.

She cringed. "It turned out to be his backyard."

"And?" Rachel encouraged, motioning with her hand for her to continue.

"And nothing. I made a complete fool of myself. I told him I planned to smell one hundred roses, and he gave me that bouquet over there by my easel, probably hoping I would leave. He knows we're booked to cater cupcakes at his brother's wedding in a few weeks, and now he's just poking fun."

"Kim's been painting roses ever since she brought back that bouquet on Friday," Andi teased. "And she's been creating roses from frosting and rolled fondant for the tops of all our cupcakes, too. Just look at the display case."

Kim glanced toward the counter. It was true.

Rachel looped an arm through hers. "I'm sorry I wasn't much help the other day. Mike and I shouldn't have been playing around in the kitchen. Let me see if I can help you discover Nathaniel's motives for sending the bouquet. How many roses did he give you?"

Kim shrugged. "Looks like two dozen."

"I read in a magazine the number of roses in a bouquet symbolizes different sentiments," Rachel said and nodded to the flowers. "Count them."

Kim pulled her arm free of Rachel's grasp and counted with her finger. "Twenty-four."

"Okay, you were right." Rachel cocked her head. "But did you know that twenty-four roses means 'thinking of you twenty-four hours a day'?"

Kim laughed. "I doubt he meant to attach any hidden meaning."

"He must know the significance of the number of roses," Rachel insisted. "He's a rosarian."

"A what?"

"A professional rose gardener," Rachel amended.

"How many roses were in the bouquet he gave you the other day?" Andi asked.

Mia and Taylor raced over to the bouquet beside Kim's easel in the back corner of the shop and began to rattle off numbers.

"One-sun, two-blue, three-bee . . ."

"Ninety, ten, eleven-teen, twelve . . ."

Kim walked toward the vase. "Thirteen."

Rachel clapped her hands together. "Thirteen red roses means 'secret admirer.'"

"I think your magazine made that up, just like the romantic horoscopes they make up for people," Kim said, touching one of the velvety soft rose petals with her finger.

"Then why did Nathaniel send thirteen and not twelve?" Andi asked, coming to Rachel's defense. "A dozen is traditional."

Kim frowned. "They were fresh cut. Maybe he over-estimated."

Rachel waved her finger at her. "You just don't want to admit he might be interested in you."

Kim shook her head and said, "I think these flowers are to thank me for giving him a good laugh, nothing more."

"Don't be so hard on yourself," Andi scolded. "There's someone out there for you."

Her sister's words were meant to comfort, but instead they emphasized the fact she *didn't* have anyone.

"You should at least call and thank him," Rachel said, handing her the phone.

Kim froze. Rachel was right. She'd have to thank him. But then, what would she say to him? Argh. She was so bad at this. Making conversation with a stranger was bad enough, but worse when it was someone she was attracted to.

Oh, no! Was she really attracted to him, or did she just find him attractive? Her hands trembled as she took the phone and punched in the number of the nursery on the card.

Yes, he was attractive. And, yes, she was attracted to him, not only because of his height, blue eyes, and warm friendly accent, but because he was as much an artist with his flowers as she was with her paints. She also liked the way he humored her.

The phone rang once . . . twice . . . three times . . . and then the message came on. Hearing his voice cross over the line as he instructed his callers to leave their name and number sent a nervous tremor of excitement up her spine.

There was a beep, and she hesitated. "Uh . . . this is Kim, Kim Burke from Creative Cupcakes. I . . . uh . . . thank you for the roses. Now I guess I'm at one hundred and thirteen, plus twenty-four, that's one hundred and thirty-seven. An odd number—"

Another beep sounded, as if warning her to stop counting and hang up the phone. Why did she jabber on like that? She could kick herself! Instead she squeezed her eyes shut and shook her head, her hope for a date with Nathaniel fading fast.

However, the roses continued to come. And Rachel continued to interpret their meaning.

On Tuesday, she received twenty roses, which meant "my feelings are sincere."

Wednesday, she received one single long-stemmed rose: "love at first sight."

Thursday, ten roses: "you are perfect."

Friday, seven roses: "I'm infatuated with you."

And Saturday, twelve roses: "be mine."

Each day, Kim called Sjölander's Garden Nursery to thank him, but Nathaniel was never there. She continued to leave messages on his answering machine, and he continued to write short notes on the delivery tags. The last one read, "See you on Sunday."

Of course, that meant no sleep for her Saturday night. How could she sleep when the anticipation of seeing him and conversing face to face loomed less than twelve hours ahead? She tried to count sheep but ended up counting the hours and then minutes. The only problem was that he never told her exactly what time he would be arriving. Would he come to the cupcake shop? Or ask her to meet him after work?

"No one sends roses to a woman every day unless he's interested," Rachel teased when they arrived for work at four on Sunday morning.

Kim rubbed the sleep from her eyes and smiled. She was beginning to believe her.

"Here come our new recruits!" Andi said, looking toward the front door.

Kim followed her gaze. A tall, lanky college-age kid with scruffy hair like Shaggy on the cartoon TV series *Scooby Doo* had just walked in behind two teenage girls.

"Rachel, Kim, I'd like you to meet Eric, Meredith, and Theresa."

Meredith had flaming red hair, far brighter, straighter, and shorter than Rachel's. She also had sharp eyes like a hawk—eyes that seemed to assess each person, as if looking for the weakest prey.

The other girl, Theresa, had blond hair so pale it made Andi's look almost brown in comparison. This girl was also stick thin, whereas Andi had a few pounds to lose.

Kim pressed her lips together. Looked like she was once again the outsider, the only one in the group who was a dark brunette.

"I'm so excited you've decided to join our team here at Creative Cupcakes," Andi said, greeting their new recruits. "Where's Heather?"

Heather walked in a second later, her eyes bloodshot and weary, her caramel hair a mess. "If we work here, are we always going to have to come in this early?"

"We work in shifts," Andi told her seventeen-year-old babysitter and her friends. "But, yes, some of us have to get here before dawn to bake all the cupcakes before we open at nine."

Rachel handed them each a pink bibbed apron to put on and a pink bandana to hold back their hair.

"Pink?" Eric drew back. "You want *me* to wear pink?"

"What would you suggest, Eric?" Andi asked, raising her brows.

"Something more manly." The boy looked down at the white T-shirt and pants Andi had instructed them to wear. "Can't I just wear white?"

Not if Andi had her way. Kim hid a smile and said, "I think we have a white apron in the kitchen closet."

Andi frowned. "What about his hair?"

"He'd look silly in a pink bandana," Rachel told her. "How about we have him wear a white baker's hat?"

"Okay," Andi agreed. "Now, let's split them up between us and show them what to do."

Andi took Eric and Theresa with her to give them a lesson on how to bake, and Rachel showed Heather the cash register, which, Kim realized, left the red-haired, hawk-eyed Meredith with *her*.

"Have you ever decorated cupcakes before?" Kim asked.

Meredith shrugged. "Of course. Hasn't everyone?"

"Well," Kim continued, giving Red Hawk a direct look. "We specialize in intricate designs created out of different consistencies of frosting and fondant. Kids like cupcakes that look like animals and sports balls. Adults like scenes painted on with food coloring or sculpted like this rose garden here."

Kim pointed to her re-creation of Nathaniel's yard. She'd joined together the tops of a dozen cupcakes with one layer of green icing and added walnut walkways and swirled vanilla roses of every color.

"No problem," Meredith said, her voice smug.

But by the time Kim turned the front window sign around to indicate Creative Cupcakes was open for business, it was clear they were in a heap of trouble. Flour, sugar, baking soda, powdered cocoa, and a variety of nuts, berries, and other toppings spilled over every counter and all over the floor.

Andi, who was OCD about kitchen safety, raced around in panic mode barking orders and trying to clean up before anyone slipped and fell.

"This is worse than the kids' cupcake camp on Tuesdays," Rachel complained.

Mia nodded. "My friends bake better than them. That girl," she said, looking at Theresa, "put too many eggs in the batter and tried to scoop one back out with a spoon. I saw her."

Taylor pointed to Eric. "He wiped crumbs on the floor and tried to lick the batter."

"Are these kids always in here?" Eric asked, narrowing his gaze toward them.

Heather laughed. "Yes, but you'll love Mia and Taylor once you get to know them."

"Heather's our favorite babysitter," Mia told him. "You should listen to her."

Eric didn't look convinced. "Can I drive the Cupcake Mobile? That would be cool."

"What would be cool is if you would stop talking and get busy sweeping," Andi said, handing him a broom.

"I can sweep," Theresa volunteered and jumped up and down, her long ponytail swinging like a propeller and threatening every bakery item on the back shelf.

When Rachel put a hand on her shoulder to stop her, the girl apologized.

"It's the sugar," Theresa declared. "The sweetness hangs in the air, making me feel like I've had five cups of coffee!"

Kim greeted the incoming customers, many of them children with their dads for Father's Day. The buy-one-get-one-free Cupcakes with Dad coupons they'd distributed during the week appeared to be a success. Jake came in to share a cupcake with Taylor, and Kim knew Andi was touched he wanted to include Mia.

Turning from their uniformed customer at the counter to the flaming redhead by her side, Kim asked, "Where's the order you boxed for Officer Lockwell? Four maple bacon–pancake cupcakes?"

Meredith threw up her hands. "Gone."

"What do you mean, 'gone'?"

The teenager looked at her as if she were stupid. "I mean, it's not here."

"Could be the Cupcake Bandit," Rachel suggested.

"The Cupcake Bandit?" Eric's eyes grew wide. "Can I try to catch him in the Cupcake Mobile?"

"I think I'm having an allergic reaction to the sugar," Theresa continued, her hair swinging out again and knocking a stack of cupcake boxes to the floor. "Oops!"

"Isn't she cute when she's all wired up?" Eric asked with a grin. "Seriously," he said to Theresa, "do you feel like you're floating? Like drifting on a cloud of sugar in space?"

"Andrea Leanne Burke," Kim hissed, pulling her

sister aside, "what were you thinking when you hired these people?"

Andi grimaced. "Heather assured me her friends would be great, and none of them had a job."

"No wonder," Kim said through gritted teeth.

"Training takes time," Andi coaxed.

"Time we don't have," Kim reminded her and moved back to the register, where Officer Lockwell waited.

"I phoned in the order at 7:30," he told her. "Isn't it ready?"

"They were boxed, but our new trainees must have misplaced them. Unless someone from the station picked the order up for you."

"No one paid for it," Andi said, opening a new box and placing his cupcakes inside. "This is the fourth order this week that has disappeared right off the counter. Seems we have a thief on our hands. You may have to patrol the shop more often, Officer Lockwell."

Their top cupcake supporter grinned. "I'd be glad to."

KIM DELIVERED A plate of cupcakes to a table in the dining area, spotted Grandpa Lewy, and motioned to Rachel.

"Grandpa, I didn't see you come in," Rachel said, walking over to his table. "Would you like a cupcake?"

"Of course!" he exclaimed. "Today is Cupcakes with Dad, and you said granddads were invited. Kim, if you let me be your dad today, I can get two cupcakes. And if Andi joins us, I can have three."

"Your doctors wouldn't approve of your eating so many sweets," Kim said, giving him a smile. "And our father just walked through the door."

William Burke sat on a stool at the cupcake counter and took the cupcake Andi offered him.

"Happy Father's Day," Kim said, pouring him a cup of coffee. She glanced at her sister. "Did you tell him?"

"Tell me what?" their father asked, giving them each a look.

Andi's face lit up as she held out her hand to show him her new ring. "Jake and I are engaged!"

"After only three months?"

Kim tensed as her father's condescending tone hit its mark, and the joy on her sister's face began to fade.

"We love each other, and I know Jake's right for me," Andi said, lifting her chin.

"Like the last one? Your deadbeat ex who ran off with his secretary to Vegas and left you and Mia high and dry?"

"Dad!" Kim protested, but he waved a hand for her to stay silent and uninvolved.

"Jake's different," Andi said, visibly struggling to keep her emotions intact. "I thought you liked Jake."

"He's a likable fellow. But you are always rushing into things and getting yourself into trouble." He shook his head. "Some things never change."

"And some things do," Andi argued, her tone now matching their father's and her face mirroring his cold, callous bitterness.

Kim had watched similar scenes unfold between the two of them in the past but never with this much clarity. Her heart felt the sting of his words as if he'd spoken them to her, and she couldn't keep silent, couldn't bear to see her sister's happiness crushed. She needed help.

"Dad, Jake is a great guy and will take care of Andi and Mia and make them very happy."

"Was I talking to you?" her father demanded.

Kim shrank back. "No, sir."

Andi shot her a look of gratitude for trying, but, like their father said, some things never changed. Least of all him.

"Well, let's hope everything works out," he muttered. "Glad Kim here isn't so crazy as to get involved with someone at the drop of a hat. She's career focused, an achiever, like all the other Burkes in our family."

Kim swallowed hard. She didn't want to be a super-achiever. And she certainly didn't want him to use her as an example for her older sister to follow. Like Andi and Rachel, she'd love to have a handsome guy claim she was the one for him and get down on one knee and propose.

She glanced at her bouquets of roses. While she wasn't sure if she'd ever get a proposal of her own, she wished she had at least a *taste* of romance.

Heather called out to her, "Hey, Kim!" Kim turned her head to see what the teenager wanted. And then she saw him: tall, blond, blue-eyed Nathaniel Sjölander. He stood at the counter opposite Heather, who motioned her toward him.

Excusing herself from her "happy" family reunion, she met Nathaniel in front of the cupcake display.

"Hello, Kimberly," he greeted. "Busy today, I see."

"Yes," she said, her nerves dancing beneath her skin. "Very busy."

"I was busy this week, too," Nathaniel told her. "I had to stay in Portland after the Rose Festival, and when I got back yesterday, my future sister-in-law insisted I go with her and my brother for the bridal party tuxedo fittings. But I enjoyed hearing your voice on my messages each night."

Kim shrugged and gave him a shy smile. "All I did was say thank you."

"Five different ways each time," he teased.

Heat surged into her cheeks. She'd tried to talk sensibly, but her words were always more fluent inside her head than when they came out of her mouth. And it didn't help now that Andi and Rachel were staring. She saw them give Nathaniel a long, appreciative perusal.

Andi gasped. "Is *that* Nathaniel?"

In a hushed voice, Rachel whispered back, "Ooh! Must be. He has an accent."

Even Heather, Theresa, and Meredith stopped what they were doing to take notice.

"I was wondering if you aren't too busy this evening, if you might want to—"

A high-pitched alarm drowned out Nathaniel and all other sounds in the shop. The double doors to the kitchen burst open, and Eric fell through, his white pants and shirt outlined by the cloud of thick black smoke behind him. With his eyes wide and his face drained of color, he shouted only one word:

"*Fire!*"

For a moment no one moved. Then all at once, the customers rushed for the door. Andi shouted for Mia and grabbed the Cupcake Diary off the counter. Rachel yanked the cash drawer out of the register.

Kim's breath caught in her chest, and her throat tightened into a chokehold. Then she exchanged a tense half-second look with Nathaniel and spun her gaze toward each wall, which were adorned with her prize-winning paintings.

She'd never save them in time.

Chapter Four

We are shaped and fashioned by what we love.

—**Johann Wolfgang von Goethe**

KIM RAN TO the wall and tried to lift a painting off its hook, but she was too short. Before she could grab a chair to stand on, two long arms reached over her head and took the artwork down for her.

Nathaniel.

"I'll get these," he said, taking a second and third painting off the wall. "Go for the lower ones."

Kim shot him a look of gratitude. "I can't replace them. They're one-of-a-kind originals."

Behind her she heard Andi order, "Rachel, prop the kitchen door open. Heather, get Mia and Taylor outside. I'll turn off the oven."

"I'm right behind you!" Jake shouted. "Careful, Andi."

Nathaniel tucked several paintings under each arm. "Where do you want them?"

Kim nodded toward the exit. "In the Cupcake Mobile out front."

While Nathaniel ran the artwork to safety, Kim jumped back to avoid the onslaught of "help" from their new recruits.

"What do we do?" Theresa squealed, spraying water from the small hand-washing sink into the air.

"I've got it," Eric announced, grabbing a fire extinguisher from the side cabinet. With a blast of roaring foam, he ran around spraying everything in the shop, including Andi when she reemerged from the kitchen.

"What, are you crazy?" Meredith yelled at them. "Let's get out of here."

Kim took her armload of paintings out to the truck, and when she ran back inside, she found Nathaniel had removed the rest.

"That's everything?"

"*Ja*, I'm quite sure."

"Please evacuate the building," a firefighter shouted, pulling her arm.

Kim crossed the street toward Andi, who stood in a huddle with Mia, Taylor, Jake, and the last person they needed to witness this debacle—their father.

"Remember the fire you set during your high school cooking class?" he demanded. "I told you opening your own bake shop was a bad idea. Everyone in Astoria is going to think you're a pyromaniac."

"I didn't set this one," Andi argued.

"Does it matter?" he taunted. "It's still your business."

"And Rachel's, Kim's, and Jake's," Andi reminded him.

"Kim would never set a fire," he retorted.

"Dad," Kim protested. "Please don't—"

"Stay out of this," her father warned. "You don't want your sister's troubles to rub off on you."

Andi gasped and walked away. Kim did the same. No amount of reasoning would make him listen. Ever. Maybe he was too afraid of what they had to say now that their mother was no longer with them to keep the peace.

Mike's car squealed to a stop across the street and Kim watched him jump out and hurry toward her. "I got a text from Rachel. Where is she?"

"Grandpa?" Rachel shouted, running through the crowd. "Has anyone seen my grandfather?"

Mike grabbed Rachel's shoulders and spun her around. "He's right there."

A firefighter had Grandpa Lewy by the arm and was escorting him from the smoking structure.

"Grandpa, where were you?" Rachel scolded.

"In the bathroom," he replied, clutching his memory box to his chest.

"I thought maybe the Cupcake Bandit had stolen you, too."

"I didn't see any bandit," Grandpa Lewy told her. "All I saw was the mailman."

"The mailman?" Kim asked, noting Nathaniel was once again by her side. "He's been in the shop every time we've had a box of cupcakes go missing and has a bag big enough to hide them in."

Rachel gasped. "Are you suggesting that a United States Postal Service worker is our cupcake thief?"

Kim pointed. "See? There he is, watching us as we speak."

Everyone turned their heads, and the mail carrier darted for his truck.

"He *is* acting suspicious," Rachel agreed.

"We need to go after him," Kim said, her voice rising. "We can't let him get away."

"I can't leave Grandpa Lewy," Rachel said, taking her grandfather's arm.

"Don't worry; I'll go," Mike assured them. "I'll catch him in the Cupcake Mobile."

"No!" Kim shook her head. "I put all of my paintings in the truck, and if you drive, they'll scrape together."

"I can drive you," Nathaniel offered.

"You can do it," Rachel encouraged.

Kim did a double take. "You want *me* to chase after the cupcake thief?"

When she'd said "we need to go after him," she hadn't meant to include herself. Confrontations weren't her forte. She never knew what to say or how to react.

"It was your idea," Mike reminded her.

Kim nodded, followed Nathaniel to his vehicle, and cast him a nervous glance. "A motorcycle?"

Nathaniel grinned and handed her a helmet. "Ever ridden one?"

She shook her head. "No."

"Now or never," he urged.

Strapping on the helmet, she climbed on the back of the bike and held on to him for dear life as he sped down the road toward the mail truck.

The driver parked in front of a house around the corner, got out, and stepped on to the sidewalk.

"Stop!" Kim hopped off the motorcycle and ran toward him. "Let me see your bag."

The mail carrier pulled the blue-gray bag tight against his side with one hand and pulled out a can of pepper spray with his other.

"Don't come any closer," he warned. "Stealing mail is a federal offense."

"We mean you no harm, nor your mail," Nathaniel said, using a good-natured tone. "We're only looking for the cupcakes that were stolen."

"Cupcakes?" The mailman looked perplexed. "You think this bag carries stolen cupcakes?"

Kim narrowed her eyes, and the mailman laughed.

"Why would I steal cupcakes?"

Kim lifted her chin. "Because everyone knows Creative Cupcakes are the best."

"They *are* the best," he admitted.

"Or maybe you overheard that we must buy the building, and for some insidious reason you don't want us to succeed."

"I cannot allow you near the contents of this bag," he said, his face serious. "Move out of my way, or I'll call the cops."

"Look. Here comes a cop now," Kim said, pointing over his shoulder.

The mail carrier swung around, and as he did, the bag slipped off his shoulder and spilled out onto the ground. He stooped to gather the contents, and to Kim's disappointment, it truly was only mail.

"Happy now?" he demanded.

Kim squeezed her eyes shut for a brief second and nodded. "Sorry for the false accusation. Next time you come by Creative Cupcakes, I'll give you a free order."

"Not the burnt ones you baked today, I hope."

"Of course not," Kim assured him.

"Creative Cupcakes has been cleared, and the fire department is allowing people back in," Officer Lockwell said as he approached. "Seems there wasn't much evidence of a fire after all, only smoke."

Just like her Cupcake Bandit theory.

WHEN NATHANIEL BROUGHT her back to Creative Cupcakes, Guy was in the process of locking his ten-speed bicycle to a chain-link fence.

"Heard about all the excitement," he said. "You girls sure like to start early. It's not even noon."

"Not even noon, and we'll be shut down the rest of the day," Kim added. "The loss of sales will hurt."

She handed her helmet back to Nathaniel, and the tattoo artist glanced at the blue body of the shiny Honda Shadow with its chrome finish and black leather seat.

"Yeah," Guy said, standing in front of his ten-speed and puffing out his chest as he gave Nathaniel an acknowledging nod. "My other bike is a Harley."

Kim laughed, but then her mood sobered when she turned toward Nathaniel. "Sorry about everything that happened today. Not what you expected when you arrived, was it?"

"No, it wasn't," he said with a grin. "A fire, a cupcake bandit, and a high-speed chase all in less than an hour. Is your life always this exciting?"

"No." Kim replied. "This isn't my idea of fun."

"What is?"

"Travel. I wish I could travel the world."

"Astoria is hosting the Scandinavian Festival next weekend. It doesn't require travel, but if you come with me, I could at least introduce you to a different culture."

A date! He asked her on a date! But Creative Cupcakes would need her now more than ever. They'd have to clean the kitchen to remove the heavy black soot the smoke left behind and work hard to recoup the financial loss from shutting down on Father's Day.

"I'm working the festival in the afternoons," Kim told him.

"So am I," he said, and an excited shine entered his eyes. "But there's the Troll Run in the morning, bright and early."

Kim wavered with indecision, the golden wings in her pocket warring with the protective Band-Aid over her heart. The Troll Run, a several-mile informal foot race through the Olney Countryside just outside of Astoria, had been on her local to-do list for years. Right above "ride a motorcycle." But was she really ready to start a new relationship? Was he?

She thought of her sister's reprimand: "Take time. Go on an adventure." And the wings won.

"Yes, I'd love to accompany you on the Troll Run," Kim said, and as their eyes locked, she believed she saw a lot of excitement in her future.

But for now, Nathaniel rode off to return to the nursery, and Kim returned to the blackened interior of the cupcake shop.

"Watch where you step," Andi warned.

Kim looked down at the floor, which was splattered with the dropped remains of cinnamon-apple cupcakes with maple syrup–cream cheese icing.

"Did you catch the mailman?" Rachel asked.

"Yes, but he isn't our thief," Kim informed her.

Andi scowled. "I wish I could find who it is. Not only was Officer Lockwell's order taken, but also the box of prepacked mixes I was going to deliver to some local stores."

"Did you check the security camera footage?" Kim suggested.

"Yes, Jake took a look at it while you were gone. All the camera caught was part of a bare arm—an elbow, to be exact, and a glimpse of pale hair. Not enough to identify a suspect. It could have been anyone. And the lighting of the camera seemed to be off. The hair color could have been white, blond, or even light brown."

"Mike is a pro at how to make things disappear from his years of performing magic tricks," Rachel added. "And he says whoever is taking our cupcakes is very quick."

"Have you talked to Mia and Taylor?" Kim asked.

"Kids can be quick. They could be taking cupcakes without realizing those orders are for other people."

Andi shook her head. "The girls wouldn't take cupcakes without asking, and they know we're looking for a thief. Right now the theft is a minor annoyance, but if this keeps up, the Cupcake Bandit may put us out of business."

"It wouldn't be the first time someone tried," Rachel reminded her. "Remember the Zumba lady and her troupe of health-conscious dancers? And what about Gaston, the French baker who claimed there can be only one cupcake shop in Astoria?"

"We should keep a list of how many batches of cupcakes we make and where we place the orders," Kim said, taking out the Cupcake Diary and making a few notes. "We should also keep a list of the disappearances—what time they occurred, what was taken, which flavors of cupcakes . . ."

Rachel laughed. "You think the Cupcake Bandit might have a favorite flavor?"

"Who knows?" Kim said and frowned as she flipped to the next page in the diary. "What's this?"

Andi's small, neat, typewriter-like handwriting read:

Tall, blond, foreign accent, nature lover (obvious because he gardens), rides cool motorcycle (implies adventure), perfect for Kim.

Rachel's signature bold block lettering added:

Three months, three girls . . . think she'll get engaged, too?

Kim looked at the smiles on Andi's and Rachel's faces and sputtered, "Nathaniel and I haven't even had a first date."

"But he did ask you to go on one, didn't he?" Rachel prodded.

"We're entering the Troll Run on Saturday," she admitted. "I had to say yes. He helped save my paintings."

Rachel gave her a teasing grin. "Of course."

Andi pulled a yellow bucket and a mop out of the corner closet. "By Saturday Creative Cupcakes should be bouncing back toward success. But right now, we have a lot of cleaning up to do."

Kim stared at the new employees, who had cost them twice their salary, lined up behind her sister, waiting for instruction. "Aren't you going to fire them? For setting the fire?"

"It wasn't me who left the cupcakes in the oven too long," Meredith protested.

"It wasn't me either," Eric said. "I was just the one who found them."

"Today was their first day," Andi told her. "We should have been watching them closer. Now, let's dish out some clean-up assignments. Eric, you take the mop."

"Wait," Eric said, glancing around at the others. "We get paid overtime for this, right?"

FINALLY FINISHED AT the end of the day, Kim went with Andi and Rachel to visit with Rachel's grandfather and take him the Father's Day cupcake he never had a chance to share with them.

"Grandpa Lewy's girlfriend, Bernice, will also be there," Rachel told them. "And she's *rich*."

"Would she finance a loan or buy the building so we can keep Creative Cupcakes?" Kim asked.

Rachel smiled. "It's worth a try."

"Oh, I hope she says yes," Andi said, crossing her fingers. "Jake put everything he could into the shop to get it started and has no more. Another investor would be a great idea."

The assisted living senior center that Rachel's grandfather had moved into a few weeks earlier resided around the block, between the new community park and Sjölander's Garden Nursery, close enough to walk. The receptionist at the front desk had them sign in, then directed them to the elevator, which they took up to his quarters.

Rachel knocked on the door, and when Grandpa Lewy let them in, they found Bernice hadn't arrived yet.

"Mom had to work today," Rachel told him. "She says she'll bring you to the house tomorrow for a home-cooked meal."

Kim watched the white-haired man sit back in his recliner, a dazed look upon his face. Some moments he was sharper than the fine point of her paintbrush, but other moments . . . nothing. After he'd reunited with Bernice last month after more than fifty years apart, much of his memory had returned, making the doctors think perhaps part of his problem was depression.

He wasn't as forgetful as he had been. The experimental treatment Bernice was paying for seemed to be working. For a while anyway. Kim knew Rachel dreaded seeing him get to the point where he didn't respond to them anymore.

"Nice place," Andi commented, sitting on the couch opposite him.

Grandpa Lewy grunted. "I don't like it here."

"It's only for a while until you get better, Grandpa," Rachel told him. "Mom can't take care of you when she has to work, and there are nurses on staff here in case—"

"Babysitters," he amended.

Kim picked up a flyer from the coffee table and read the schedule. "The center offers a lot of fun activities."

"Feels like prison."

Rachel smirked. "You've never been to prison. And you aren't confined here. You are free to come and go as you please. The cupcake shop is only a block away. You can come and visit me anytime."

"Did you bring me a cupcake?" he asked, motioning to the small box she held in her hands.

Rachel smiled. "Yes. I don't think your nurse would approve, but I sneaked you in one anyway."

"Thank you, Rachel."

Rachel patted his arm. "Anytime, Grandpa."

"I have no friends here," he said, placing the small box next to his larger memory box covered in photos.

A knock sounded on the door, and Kim let Bernice in. "Here comes a friend for you," she told Rachel's grandfather.

Grandpa Lewy's face lit up. "She looks familiar. Who is she?"

"Someone who loves you," Rachel told him and smiled at Bernice. "We are *all* so glad you're here."

After Rachel told Bernice they needed help to buy the shop, the old woman shook her head.

"I'm sorry," she told them. "I admire you girls for going after your dreams and opening the cupcake shop, and God knows your grandpa loves cupcakes, but I need to save what money I've got to pay for Lewy's treatments. Medical expenses aren't cheap, and we have no idea how long he'll need care."

"I know," Rachel told her. "My mom and I appreciate what you're doing for him."

As THE DOOR shut behind them on their way out, Kim couldn't help but think that even Grandpa Lewy had someone special who cared for him. Her thoughts turned toward Nathaniel, especially since they had to walk past his yard on their way back.

Andi caught her glancing toward the black wrought iron gate. "So are you looking forward to it?"

"To what?" Kim asked, feigning innocence.

"Your date with the handsome Swede," Andi teased.

Kim shrugged. "He's nice. It will be okay. I'll be fine."

"Of course you'll be fine," Rachel said, in her infectious sing-song voice. "About time you took a chance on love again. And what's better than a rose gardener who can send you roses every day?"

"I wonder how many you'll get tomorrow," Andi mused.

Kim smiled. "Okay, yes, I'm looking forward to it."

"What part?" Rachel teased. "The date or the roses?"

"All of it," Kim admitted and continued to smile all the way to the shop and all the way home.

Chapter Five

The best and most beautiful things in the world cannot be seen or even touched—they must be felt with the heart.

—Helen Keller

KIM PULLED THE ribbon-tied bundle of seven different species of flowers from beneath her pillow. Did it work? The Scandinavian street vendor she'd met at the bonfire the night before had assured her if she slept on the flowers on Midsummer's Eve, her future husband would appear to her in a dream.

She'd dreamed of Nathaniel but wasn't sure if it was just wishful thinking. Dropping the flowers on her nightstand, she threw on a green tank top to match the color of her eyes and a pair of faded denim cut-offs for the Troll Run.

Her gaze swung to the bulletin board on her wall with the maps, postcards, and brochures she'd collected of various places she wanted to go but would never see because they all required an airplane flight.

She knew she should remove the photos and other travel paraphernalia so they wouldn't taunt her. But that wouldn't stop her from imagining herself walking the streets outside Buckingham Palace, or horseback riding across the green Irish countryside, or climbing into a Venetian gondola. No, taking away the items wouldn't take away her dreams any more than taking away a framed photo could take away her memories of her mother.

She reached out and picked up a photo of her mother standing beside her at the Port of Astoria West Basin Marina. It was the last one taken before her mom's small-engine plane crash.

There was a knock on her bedroom door, and a moment later, Andi entered the room.

"Look at this article Jake wrote for the paper," her sister said, handing her a copy of the *Astoria Sun*. "He tells about the fire and our thefts and has asked the public to help us identify the notorious 'Cupcake Bandit.'"

"Do you think it will draw people into Creative Cupcakes to search for our thief?" Kim asked.

"Well, it's a better idea than chasing down our mailman," Andi teased. "I still can't believe you did that. Usually, I'm the impulsive one. Must have had something to do with Nathaniel offering you a ride on his motorcycle."

"I wasn't thinking," Kim admitted. "The chaos with the fire, then the threat of losing all my paintings . . ."

"And the fact Nathaniel showed up," Andi added with a grin, "all worked together to discombobulate your sensible head?"

Kim nodded and set the photo of their mother down. "The anniversary of Mom's crash always drives me a little crazy, too. Next week marks ten years."

"I wish she could see us now, see Mia, and be at the wedding," Andi said, her voice soft. "Jake and I have decided to get married in September."

"That gives me three months to find my own apartment," Kim said, "or I'll be sleeping in the Cupcake Mobile."

Andi laughed. "Guy said he did that before he opened his tattoo parlor and sold the truck to us."

"Not that I'd like to share his fate," Kim said, and she meant the words in more ways than one.

While sleeping in a drafty, rattling, antique hunk of metal on wheels would not be fun, going through life until she was old and gray without ever a taste of romance seemed far worse.

NATHANIEL LOOKED FANTASTIC in his navy blue T-shirt and gray-striped board shorts. She should have pinned him as more of the surfer-adventurer type than the kind that works out in a gym.

When he'd arrived in front of Andi's small Victorian cottage on the hill to pick her up, his approval rating had skyrocketed in her heart higher than any of the previous men she'd ever dated, including Gavin.

First, Gavin had never sent her roses. Second, he *was* the type who may have bought gym shorts. Third, his smile could never have out radiated the one on Nathaniel's face when he looked at her.

Goodbye, Gavin; hello, Nathaniel.

To top off what was sure to be one of the most glorious days of her life, the sun was rising over the Columbia River without a single cloud to block its path.

"Thank you for coming with me," Nathaniel greeted her.

"Thank you for asking," she replied.

Nathaniel grinned. "Thank you for giving me the chance to ask."

"No motorcycle today?" she asked, glancing toward his truck parked at the curb.

"The pickup is better to transport the rosebushes to the festival," he said. "And as delightful as it is to have you hold on to me from behind, I'd prefer you sitting beside me where I can look at you."

The Annual Running of the Trolls started at 8:30 a.m. from the Clatsop County Fairgrounds parking lot. They had chosen the 5.75-mile run over the shorter 1.5- and 3-mile paths to stretch out their time together before they'd both have to work the festival later that afternoon.

"No fair," Kim said, her voice coming out in a rasp. "Your legs are twice as long as mine."

"I could pick you up and carry you," he teased.

"Let's walk."

"And chance being caught by a wandering troll? I've heard they can be quite nasty."

"I thought trolls were afraid of sunlight," she countered.

"*Ja*, but they still roam the shady forests."

"I trust you'll protect me from being eaten," she said, as they slowed their pace.

"Eaten? No, they won't eat you. On Midsummer's Day they'll club you and torture you into giving up your pickled herring, boiled potatoes, and strawberry cakes."

Kim laughed. "Maybe in Sweden, but I have yet to see a troll in the Astoria–Warrenton area. How long have you lived here?"

"A year. I followed my brother. He came to the States and bought a house near our cousins. He urged me to visit, and when I did, I, too, decided to extend my stay. Sjölander's Garden Nursery opened five months later and has seen steady business ever since."

"The roses are beautiful," she told him.

He grinned at her again. "As are you."

Kim didn't know what to say. She'd never mastered the knack of flirting with men, like Rachel, or challenging men, like Andi.

All she could do was continue to smile and say, "Thank you."

AFTER THEY RETURNED to the Clatsop Fairgrounds and crossed the finish line, Nathaniel made her promise to meet him during her lunch break at the Scandinavian Festival later that afternoon. "At vendor space number eight," he insisted. Then he drove her home so she could shower before she had to help Rachel and Andi load cupcakes into the Cupcake Mobile.

"How did it go?" Andi asked when she arrived at the shop.

"We had to dodge the Viking encampment and the downtown Op Tog walking parade while driving back," she confided. "And I think we almost hit a troll."

"Sounds like you had fun."

"I had an adventure," Kim agreed. "How are things here?"

Andi gave her a pensive look. "Sam Warden heard about the fire. He said if we can't buy the building by July first, we need to leave. He won't let us stay longer even if the building hasn't sold by then."

Kim thought of her latest creations, sculpted from icing to decorate the tops of the cupcakes for the festival. "Let's hope we sell lots of cupcakes today."

A short while later the Creative Cupcakes booth was up and running. Kim served magically minty grasshopper cupcakes and vanilla cupcakes with whipped cream and fresh sliced strawberries on top. She had cupcakes sculpted like trolls with big bulbous noses and pointy green hats. Cupcakes with wreaths of flowers. And cupcakes with large individual roses.

"Meredith, that's incredible!" Andi exclaimed. "I didn't realize you were so talented."

Kim turned her head and caught the look on the teenager's arrogant face. Was Meredith trying to take credit for *her* work?

"I decorated them," Kim corrected her sister. "Meredith mixed the different colors for the icing."

Andi gave Meredith a questioning glance.

Meredith shrugged and replied, "I could have decorated them just as well."

Kim narrowed her eyes. If she didn't know better, she'd think the teen had read her mind, knew she'd considered leaving, and aimed to replace her.

"These cupcakes look exactly like a plate of vegetables," Andi crooned. "So real I wouldn't even know it was cake."

"Wait until you see my plate of spaghetti and meatball cupcakes," Kim said, bringing them out to show her. "I used a fork to carve the frosting into spaghetti, round chocolate mini cakes for the meatballs, and raspberry syrup poured over the top for the sauce."

"Not good for my diet," Andi warned. "You'll make me want to eat them all."

"I agree," said a plump woman stepping up to their booth. "I'll buy both sets."

"I'll take this tray of cupcakes decorated like a rose garden," another lady told them. "I've never seen such artistic work."

Kim warmed to the praise and gave her wannabe rival, Meredith, another glance. Maybe using her artistic skills to decorate cupcakes could bring her as much satisfaction as painting. Maybe if Creative Cupcakes remained in business, she wouldn't need a replacement.

However, five hours later, she admitted she could use what Nathaniel termed a "*fika* break." Sales had brought in more money than at any previous event they'd participated in. The line of customers was twenty deep, and Kim had been selling and serving cupcakes every second.

Andi switched with Rachel halfway through the day so she could take Mia back to the cupcake shop and Rachel could bring Grandpa Lewy and Mike to the festival.

Kim glanced at the old man as Rachel led him toward their white, twelve-by twelve foot tented booth. He looked exceptionally pale, and his mouth was tight-lipped and grim.

"Are you feeling okay?" she asked.

"Can you bring me that thing I like to sit on?" he responded.

"A chair?" she asked.

He nodded, and Kim guided him toward a seat at the back of the tent.

"I'm worried about him," Rachel whispered to her. "He hasn't spoken much today."

"Are you sure you'll manage here without me?" Kim asked.

Rachel waved her off. "Go have fun."

Kim felt a flutter in her stomach, but it didn't have anything to do with hunger. She couldn't wait to see Nathaniel again.

She hurried past the other outdoor vendors and counted off their numbered spaces as she went by. He'd said he had something special planned, something to do with his brother's business, although she'd failed to ask what that was. She knew he had set up a booth selling his prize-winning roses.

Five ... six ... seven ... space number eight. She looked up from the spray-painted number on the ground and spotted Nathaniel holding a picnic basket and a bottle of wine. And there behind him was an enormous red-and-yellow hot air balloon.

She froze, her stomach taking a ninety-degree dive straight into a pool of dread. Did he intend to take her up off the ground in that thing ... and *fly?*

Chapter Six

Life is a daring adventure or nothing at all.

—Helen Keller

"WHAT'S WRONG?" NATHANIEL asked, his smile fading as she drew closer. "Are you afraid of heights?"

"No," she said, each step toward him heavier than the next. "I'm afraid of *flying*."

He gave her a hesitant half-grin. "Are you sure you don't want to even try?"

Her gut wrenched with indecision. Nathaniel had looked so excited when he first saw her. She glanced at the open picnic basket that he had placed on the ground by his feet and saw sandwiches, red grapes, cinnamon rolls, and two plastic glasses.

Dear God, she didn't want to disappoint him, didn't

want to ruin things between them before they even got started. Kim looked from him to the balloon, then back to the hope in his beautiful blue eyes.

He pulled away from her gaze and shrugged. "I'm sorry, I didn't know. I got the idea when I carried one of your paintings out to the Cupcake Mobile during the fire. The painting of the sky full of balloons, with the girl on the ground reaching out her hand as if yearning to fly over the trees and set off on a grand adventure of her own."

Kim stared at him. "That's exactly how I felt when I painted it."

"Then what's stopping you?"

"My mother. She died in a plane crash when I was seventeen, and my plans to travel the world crashed with her. I tried to board a plane after college. I got my passport, bought my ticket, walked up the boarding ramp . . . and I panicked. All the memories of my mother's death came flooding back, and I couldn't go on."

"So you fear your own death?"

"I fear being hurt," Kim said, and tried to swallow the painful memory. "She . . . didn't die right away."

"This is my brother's balloon," Nathaniel told her. "At festivals we take people up a hundred feet, but the balloon stays tethered to the ground the whole time. We don't have to go up in the balloon if you don't want." He shrugged. "We can have our picnic right here on the ground among the other people waiting to get eaten by trolls."

Kim smiled and looked up at the balloon again. How she did yearn to fly!

"Maybe we could have our picnic in the basket while it's tethered to the ground?" she asked. "Or . . . as long as it's still held by a rope, we could lift off the ground just a little bit? Like, maybe only a few feet?"

The enormous smile Nathaniel gave her erased her doubts over the suggestion, and he replied, "*Ja*, we could do that."

Taking Nathaniel's hand, she climbed into the wicker basket connected to the balloon above by a series of strong cables. The basket was large enough to hold six-teen people and open enough to keep her from feeling claustrophobic. If she wanted to, she could climb over the side and jump out any time she wished.

Nathaniel sat beside her on a portable box with the picnic basket between them. Kim discovered the bottle she'd seen in his hand earlier wasn't wine, but champagne.

"Is this a champagne brunch?" she inquired.

Nathaniel took the bottle, popped the cork, and poured her a glass. "When people first began ballooning, the balloonist would carry champagne to soothe angry or frightened spectators at the landing site."

Kim smiled. "Perfect for me."

"These days a champagne toast is tradition upon land-ing," he told her. "But since we aren't going anywhere, we might as well have some now." Raising his glass, he said, "To soft winds and gentle landings."

And to soft, gentle kisses. Kim glanced at his mouth. She wouldn't mind if he kissed her.

"Nathaniel—does everyone call you Nathaniel, or do you go by Nat or Nate?"

"They call me Nathaniel. To reduce the name my parents chose for me would dishonor them."

Kim took a sip of champagne and smiled. "Why? Are you part of royalty or something?"

He laughed and shook his head. "No. Not royalty. But my mother couldn't love me any more than the most upstanding person, and this is how I show her respect."

Kim raised her brows. "I never thought about it like that. Everyone I know uses nicknames. Seems easier in a fast-paced world."

"What is your full name?" he asked.

"Kimberly Nicole Burke."

"Doesn't anyone in your family use your full name?"

"My mother did."

"And your father?"

Kim smirked. "He doesn't call me much of anything, and when he does, it's Kim. My father likes to keep things short."

"And sweet?" Nathaniel prompted.

"No, just short," Kim corrected. "My relationship with him . . . is difficult."

"Kimberly is a beautiful name. I like it very much."

He leaned close enough to take her breath away, and her heart pounded in her chest. But no kiss.

"Would you like to go higher? Ten feet?" he asked, his hands already on the burner, ready to pump the flame.

She nodded and gripped the edge of the box on which she was sitting. "Yes, I'm ready."

Nathaniel worked the burner and the fan, which directed the hot air from the short bursts of flame into the gaping mouth of the balloon. To Kim's surprise, a thrill of excitement instead of fear shot through her, and when she looked at Nathaniel, she couldn't stop smiling.

"I've always wanted to go up in a hot air balloon," Kim admitted, pulling herself over to the edge and gripping the cable attached to the balloon. "Do you want to go higher?"

Nathaniel's eyes sparkled. "Do you?"

"At least to twenty-five feet," she suggested.

The balloon lifted, and a great weight she didn't even know she had been carrying seemed to lift with it, leaving her light and bubbly. Could it be the champagne? Doubtful. She hadn't even finished one glass.

"Oh, Nathaniel, isn't it wonderful? Imagine flying over the hillside, past the cupcake shop, and across the Columbia River to the other side. Imagine the sights we could see!"

"You don't have to imagine, Kimberly. Some sights were meant to be seen firsthand." He tied the rope to secure them at twenty-five feet and came back to sit beside her. "I could tell you about my homeland in Sweden, but if you were to go there and see it with your own eyes . . . well, it's a different thing altogether."

She thought of her bulletin board in her room filled with pictures of all the places she'd like to travel. Thought of the empty pages of her blank passport, which she had renewed and kept current . . . just in case.

Finishing the champagne, she handed him her glass and took the delicious-smelling gourmet beef and cheese sandwich on golden crusted bread he held out to her.

"It must be hard for you to be so far away from the rest of your family," she said and took a bite of the sandwich.

"My parents are coming for my brother's wedding, and then I'll be leaving with them for home three days later."

Kim coughed, sputtered, but managed to squeeze out the words "You're *leaving*?"

Maybe it was better if he didn't kiss her. She didn't need a repeat of the past, didn't need Nathaniel to leave her behind like Gavin. Sitting at the airport. Waving goodbye. *Alone.*

"How long will you stay?" she asked and set the sandwich down in her lap.

"Forever if my mother has anything to do with it." Nathaniel shook his head and gave her a rueful grin. "My mother never wanted me to come here in the first place."

"What about your roses?" she asked. "Sjölander's Garden Nursery?"

"My brother will take care of her," he said and smiled. "Now, what do you think of your first balloon flight?"

Kim's stomach churned. "I—I think I need you to take me down."

Nathaniel frowned. "Just a moment ago I saw the excitement in your eyes, heard the longing for adventure in your voice. I don't think you're afraid of flying, Kimberly. I think you're afraid to fly, to let go, to take hold of your dreams. Perhaps afraid of where they will take you."

She wouldn't look at him, wouldn't let his warm, lilting, musical voice penetrate her heart. "That's ridiculous."

"Is it?" Drawing her close, he brushed his mouth against hers and kissed her.

Kim resisted at first, but his lips were so soft and gentle, that her eyes closed, and she found herself lost in a world of enchantment, of wonder, bursting through the air, soaring . . . flying . . . higher and higher.

"Open your eyes," he whispered, holding her tight.

She opened her eyes slowly, her lashes fluttering against her skin. Then she looked up into his face, just inches from her own, and her heart signaled she'd just taken the trip of a lifetime.

"Don't hate me," he said, his mouth twitching as if to hide a smile. "But I may have let the rope slip a bit further."

Kim glanced around her and tightened her grip around his waist. "We're high. Like, fifty feet high!"

"More like seventy-five."

Kim gasped. And smiled. And laughed. "I'm *flying*."

"I love your passion, Kimberly. You put your passion into everything you do. It's in the way you paint, the way you decorate your cupcakes, and . . ." He grinned, his mouth drawing near hers again. "It's also in the way you kiss."

She prepared to kiss Nathaniel again, when a sharp ring sounded from her pocket. Her cell phone.

Nathaniel drew back, and she answered the call, hoping she hadn't lost track of the time. Had she been gone from the cupcake stand for more than an hour?

"Grandpa Lewy is missing!" Rachel shouted through the phone. "He was sitting in the chair behind me, and then he was gone. I left Meredith in charge of the booth, and Mike and I have been all over the place but can't find him. Where are you?"

"I'm up in a balloon."

"A what?"

"A hot air balloon."

There was a pause on the other end, then Rachel asked, "You're kidding, right?"

Kim laughed. "No, I'm serious."

"I'll need details later," Rachel said, "but right now I need to find my grandfather. Can you see him?"

Kim looked about and whispered to Nathaniel, "Rachel's grandfather is lost. Can we go up higher so I can try to spot him?"

Nathaniel nodded and took them up to one hundred feet. They peered down at the crowd below, hoping to spot the old man, but it was hard to tell one person from another. Then Kim saw a man with white hair holding a box close to his chest. "Rachel, I see him," she said into the phone. "He's over by the Polka Chicks, sitting on a bench, east of the cupcake stand."

"I'm on my way. Thanks, Kim."

Kim put her phone away and turned toward Nathaniel.

"I need to get back," she told him.

"Can I see you tomorrow?" he asked.

Another date, another kiss, another heartbreak when he left her for Sweden. She shouldn't make the inevitable even worse. She shouldn't say yes.

"Yes?"

She nodded. Common sense told her she should decline, but it looked like her heart had a different plan.

KIM RETURNED TO the Creative Cupcakes booth to find Rachel screaming at Meredith.

"What happened?" Kim asked, eyeing Meredith's belligerent expression.

Rachel swept her arm toward the back of the tent. "The cupcakes are gone!"

Kim glanced at the empty table where they'd stacked the dozens of cupcake boxes they'd unloaded from the Cupcake Mobile earlier that morning.

"We were pretty busy. Are you sure we didn't sell them all?" she asked.

Rachel shook her head. "When I left to find my grandpa, there were still thirty dozen boxes on the table. Meredith only sold eight dozen during that time. That means twenty-two dozen cupcakes are missing. How could Meredith not notice someone lifting the flap and stealing from the back of the tent?"

"I was too busy to notice," Meredith shot back. "With both you and Kim gone, I was the only one here to serve. You shouldn't have left me here alone."

Kim glanced from one fiery redhead to the other, and guilt crept up her spine. If she hadn't been with Nathaniel and had stayed to help Meredith, this never would have happened. There was no way twenty-two dozen cupcakes would have gone missing under *her* watch.

"Hey, great cupcakes," a young man said as he walked

by. He took a bite of a cannoli cupcake with a Swedish red candy fish on top. "Tastes fantastic!"

"I didn't sell him any cupcakes," Meredith said, her eyes wide. "He could be the thief."

"Where did you get that box?" Rachel demanded, stepping toward him. "You didn't pay us for them."

"I got them from the troll," the man said with a grin. "He said everyone had to try one."

"Troll?" Kim demanded. "What troll?"

Rachel pursed her lips. "Maybe a troll followed you from the race."

"The guy said he was a troll," the young man replied, giving them both a mischievous grin.

"Wait!" Kim shouted, running after him. But he had disappeared in the crowd. Then she realized that several other people around her were eating their cupcakes.

"Excuse me," she asked an older woman. "Where did you get that cupcake?"

"A handsome man gave it to me," the woman told her.

Handsome? They had a handsome thief who claimed he was a troll?

"What did he look like?" she persisted.

"He was tall," the woman answered.

The next woman Kim stopped said, "He was short. He went that way."

Kim ran down the path in the direction the woman indicated and came across more and more people eating Creative Cupcakes.

A group of kids laughed when Kim asked about the cupcakes, and one of them said, "The troll had white hair and a beard and a pointy green hat. He was fierce and ugly and handed us the cupcakes and ran away."

A mother with two young children told her, "He was such a nice man. Very kind. Not many people do good deeds for others anymore."

"What do you mean by 'good deeds'?"

"When I told him we didn't have any money, he gave us the cupcakes for free."

Kim returned to the Creative Cupcakes tent and discovered the Cupcake Mobile had left.

"Mike drove Grandpa Lewy home and went to get us more cupcakes," Rachel told her. "Did you learn anything about our thief?"

Kim nodded. "People described him as tall, short, handsome, ugly, young, old, in human form, and a troll. One woman referred to him as Robin Hood."

"Because he steals from the rich and gives to the poor?" Rachel asked. "Our cupcakes are rich, but we'll be poor now that he's given our cupcakes away."

Kim hesitated. "He didn't give them all away. He sold most of them . . . and pocketed our money."

Chapter Seven

Stolen kisses are always sweetest.

—Leigh Hunt

"SOMEONE TOOK CASEY!" Mia cried, running across the tile floor of the cupcake shop.

Kim watched the tears roll down her niece's cheeks and she dropped down on one knee in front of the child to console her. "Where did you last see your doll?"

Mia looked around, as if puzzled. "I don't know."

"You had Casey with you yesterday at the festival," Andi said, coming around the counter. "Did you leave her there?"

Mia's big blue eyes welled with more tears. "I don't know."

Andi glanced toward Jake's daughter, Taylor, who

was coloring with crayons at a table by the front window. "Taylor, did you take Mia's doll?"

Taylor shook her head. "No."

"Must be the bandit," Mia said, her lower lip wobbling.

Taylor agreed. "The Cupcake Bandit."

"Should we offer a reward?" Kim suggested. "A free box of cupcakes to whoever finds and returns Casey."

Mia nodded.

"If you and Taylor draw reward posters, I'll hang them up in the shop," Kim told her.

The little girl dashed off to sit at the table with Taylor, and Andi brought them two pieces of white paper.

"That will keep them busy for a while," Andi said with a grin.

"Long enough for us to load the Cupcake Mobile for the festival," Kim agreed. "Where's Rachel?"

"Right here," Rachel sang, ushering her grandfather through the front door. "Had to take Gramps to the doctor's. He had a fever this morning. My mom's coming by to get him in ten minutes."

Rachel seated him at a front table near the door by the girls, then noticed the new vase of roses on the counter. "Well, well, Kim. What have we here?"

Kim rolled her eyes as Rachel counted the stems.

"Nathaniel sent six red roses. That means, 'I want to be yours,'" Rachel teased.

"It doesn't mean anything. Nathaniel isn't looking for a relationship. He's—" Kim took a deep breath and steeled herself against their pity. "He's going back to Sweden."

"I'm so sorry," Andi said, her voice barely audible.

Kim nodded and turned away, unable to look at her. "It's okay, really. I've got my job here . . . for at least two more weeks. And I've got my painting."

"I really like this new one," Rachel said, pointing to the fresh canvas on the easel.

The picture she'd painted of two people holding hands and looking up at the stars.

Kim squeezed her eyes shut for a moment, trying to block out the image, but Nathaniel's face appeared instead. How could he leave when she'd just found him? It all seemed so unfair.

"I finished!" Mia called out and held up her colored paper. "Hang up my reward poster, Aunt Kim."

She retrieved a roll of tape and was in the middle of attaching the poster to the front window when something hit the glass with a sharp bang.

"What was that?" Taylor asked.

"A bird," Mia said, pressing her face against the pane. "I think it's dead."

Kim took an empty cupcake box off the back counter and went outside, followed by Mia and Taylor. The little blackbird hadn't died, but instead appeared stunned and was on its side. When it righted itself and tried to fly, it fell back down.

"The bird's alive," she told them. "Just a hurt wing. In a few days our feathered friend will fly as good as new."

"Are you sure?" Mia asked.

No, she wasn't sure. She wasn't sure of anything anymore. In fact, she'd felt as dazed as this little bird ever since

Nathaniel told her he was going away. Would she ever meet another person with an adventurous spirit who connected with nature and made her smile as much as he did?

Gently, Kim picked up the bird and placed it in the box, then walked back with it into the shop.

"You're bringing that thing in here?" Andi asked, her eyes wide. "What about germs?"

"I'll keep it in the box by the side door in the back party room," Kim said, carrying the bird across the room.

Mia and Taylor followed, squealing with delight.

ANDI'S SQUEALS LATER that afternoon were of a different kind, more like a burst of outrage. She held up the Cupcake Diary. "The thief left a ransom note."

Rachel looked up from the tray of red velvet cupcakes she had just brought out from the kitchen. "In our Cupcake Dairy?"

"The diary was missing since this morning, and I was afraid maybe the Cupcake Bandit stole that, too. But I just found it here on the end of the counter with this written inside."

Kim walked over by Andi and read the note aloud, squinting to decipher the poor handwriting:

I have a doll. Astoria Column. 6:30. Bring the cupcakes. Chocolate.

"Does he mean 6:30 today?" Andi asked, turning the book around to read the note again.

Kim shrugged. "He doesn't mention any other day."

A half hour after Andi called his private number, Officer Ian Lockwell entered the shop. Andi showed him the note and explained how Mia's doll had gone missing.

"I'm afraid I can't write a report over a missing toy," Officer Lockwell told them. "Or order a stakeout."

"But if he shows up to exchange the doll for the cupcakes, we can catch him," Andi insisted. "And find out who he is."

"I'm sorry," Officer Lockwell told them. "The person who took Mia's doll and the thief who stole your cupcakes might not be the same person. Plus, you have to think—what kind of crazy person would do something like this? Sounds to me like a child."

"The video showed pale hair and the elbow of an adult," Andi argued. "And the people at the Scandinavian Festival said it was a man. He was selling the cupcakes for money."

Officer Lockwell sighed. "I'm working at the station tonight, and there's no way the department is going to invest precious money or manpower to catch a dollnapper."

"Someone's got to take the cupcakes to the column," Andi said, lifting her chin. "Except Rachel and I have to head back to the festival. We told Heather and Theresa we'd be back with the next load of cupcakes ASAP."

Kim watched her sister turn toward her and gasped. "Why are you looking at me?"

"You're the only one who can do it," Rachel told her. "You need to go on a recon mission to catch our cupcake thief."

"I—I can't go alone." She shook her head. "I'm not the type to hide in the bushes and scout out criminals."

"You don't have to go alone," said a smooth, friendly voice behind her. "I'll go with you."

She spun around. How did Nathaniel manage to sneak up behind her?

Andi and Rachel clapped their hands, and each gave her a big smile.

"Sounds like a plan," Rachel said and gave her a knowing look. "Be sure to take a blanket. The air might be cool tonight."

Kim rolled her eyes. Rachel was a blatant matchmaker who didn't know when to stop.

"I have a blanket in the saddlebag of my motorcycle," Nathaniel told her.

"You brought your motorcycle?" Kim asked, unable to keep her excitement out of her voice.

"I thought you might like another taste of adventure," he said and grinned as he took her hand.

KIM HELD THE binoculars up to her eyes. The box containing a dozen chocolate cupcakes with creamy chocolate icing sat on the stone bench near the hedges toward the back side of the Astoria Column. The ransom note had not said where to put them, and she thought if she chose a place in the open, the thief wouldn't make the exchange.

"It's 6:30," Nathaniel whispered. "The Cupcake Bandit should be here any minute."

"Do you think he saw us cross the parking lot and climb the column?" Kim asked.

Nathaniel shook his head. "We were here over an hour early, he doesn't know me, and I doubt he'd recognize you."

Kim glanced down at the black leather motorcycle jacket Nathaniel had given her to hide her white work shirt. The jacket was about five sizes too big, but she didn't care. It smelled like him—like warm summer rain and happiness.

"We can see if he takes the cupcakes, but we'll never climb down fast enough to catch him," Nathaniel told her.

"That's okay," Kim said, looking down at the people wandering around on the lawn below. "I don't want to confront him. I just want to see who it is."

There were 164 steps to the top of the Astoria Column on Coxcomb Hill, where a square, railed platform let viewers oversee not only the site's thirty acres, but the entire region. Kim loved the historic frontier banded murals circling the column that Italian immigrant artist Attilo Pusterla had created using a technique combining painting and plaster carving.

"It's like the top of a lighthouse," Nathaniel commented. "And just as windy. The view reminds me of Sweden, with all the green valleys and waterways in between."

Kim swung her gaze from the huge cargo ships traveling under the massive steel truss Astoria–Megler Bridge on her right, around the piers lining the tip of Astoria, and followed Youngs Bay around to the flats of green, with trees and subtle rolling hills in the distance.

"My home city of Göteborg is a lot like Astoria," he continued. "Your town sits on the mouth of the Columbia River where it meets the Pacific Ocean, and mine sits on the mouth of Göta älv, which flows into the North Sea. Also, like Astoria, Göteborg is a thriving fishing community. I think you'd like it there."

Was he asking her to go to Sweden? Nathaniel turned toward her, and her pulsed raced. What was she supposed to say?

"There are many art galleries in Sweden," he told her, his eyes sparkling. "Including the Göteborg Museum of Art."

"And rose gardens?" she prompted, loving the sound of his accent as he talked.

"*Ja*, before I came here, I worked in the rose garden in Trädgårdsföreningen park, with four thousand roses of nineteen hundred species." He grinned. "A lot more to smell than in my backyard."

Kim smiled at his teasing and took another glance at the stone bench to make sure the cupcake box was still there. It was.

"No wonder you want to go back," she replied.

"I want to go lots of places," Nathaniel said, smiling down at her. "But I've discovered it's more fun traveling with someone than traveling alone."

Kim stared at him for several long seconds, wishing she could travel the world with him, pack her hobo bag and her paintbrushes, and fly off to other countries, immerse herself in other cultures, and capture their essence on canvas. But her gut clenched into a tight ball at the thought of the airplane flights a dream like that would require.

Avoiding Nathaniel's expectant gaze, she lifted the binoculars to her eyes. No thief on the horizon.

"I dated an Irish guy in college," she said, her voice raw. "After graduation he asked me to fly off to Ireland with him. But I thought of my mother, crashing in the wilds of Idaho with my aunt and uncle in their plane, and I . . . I couldn't go. He left me behind and flew off without me."

Nathaniel nodded, as if he understood her dilemma. "I dated a girl in college who asked me to stay. She didn't have the spirit of adventure in her and asked me to give up mine. I couldn't do it. Giving up who you are and who you are meant to be, giving up on your dreams, is a fate worse than—"

He looked at her and broke off before finishing, but Kim knew what he was going to say. *"Giving up on your dreams is a fate worse than death."* Suddenly she knew she had to change.

"Can you take me up in your brother's hot air balloon again?" she asked. "This time without the ropes tying it to the ground?"

"I could, if that's what you want. Or if you're willing to try something else, he has a seaplane that can fly low to the water to make you feel safe."

"I'd like to try," she told him. "I don't always want to be afraid to fly. Someday, when I'm ready, I'd like to actually use my passport."

"Maybe when that day comes, you'll visit Sweden," he suggested.

"Maybe," she said and drew in her breath as his mouth drew near. "Nathaniel, we can't let ourselves get distracted. We need to be on the lookout for the thief."

He pulled back. "*Ja*, you're right. I don't know what I was thinking except that you're so very cute when your eyes are wide with anticipation."

"Me?" She gasped. "You think I anticipate—"

"I find it very exciting," he assured her and drew toward her once again.

This time she didn't protest. Okay, he was right. She had been struggling with the anticipation of his kiss the entire time he'd been talking to her.

His mouth covered her lips with sweet promise, exhilarating temptation, and filled her with an intense urge to fly over the moon. Never had she lost her senses over a man so completely, not even with Gavin, whom she'd thought was the love of her life.

Now she wondered if she wasn't hurt so much by the idea that he had left her, but by the idea that he had left her behind. While he flew off to another country, she remained stuck in Astoria, where she feared she'd remain forever.

Kim reached her arms up to wrap around Nathaniel's neck and draw him closer. Then she abruptly tore her lips from his and scanned the area below. "What about the cupcake thief?"

Nathaniel glanced at his watch, shook his head, and smiled. "I don't think he's coming."

Chapter Eight

I wonder what fool it was that first invented
kissing.

—Jonathan Swift

"WHAT DO YOU mean, he didn't show?" Andi demanded.
"How are we going to get Mia's doll back?"

"Trolls are known to run off with babies," Guy inter-
jected. "Maybe he mistook the doll for the real thing."

"Let's leave a pair of size fourteen work boots outside our door," Rachel suggested. "I read in a magazine
it deters burglars if they think there's a giant inside the
premises."

"Makes sense," the tattoo artist agreed. "A short little
troll would be afraid of a giant."

Kim shot them each a look to let them know she

thought they were crazy. "I doubt our thief is a real troll. And if we put a pair of boots outside our door, any poor person off the street would take them thinking we are offering them for free."

"So how do we catch him?" Andi asked.

"Ink," Guy said, his tone matter-of-fact. "You place an exploding dye pack under the cupcake box and leave it on the end of the counter as bait. When he steals the box and tries to head out the door, a radio transmitter triggers the pack, and it explodes, marking your culprit."

"I've heard of that before," Rachel said with a nod. "Banks use it to catch robbers all the time."

"But how do we get an ink pack?" Kim asked their neighbor. "Your tattoo shop?"

"No." Guy told them and grinned. "Ebay."

TUESDAY EVENING, KIM left Creative Cupcakes two hours early for a sunset seaplane trip with Nathaniel. She glanced at him beside her in the small cockpit, and he gave her a quick kiss for reassurance.

"You know how to swim?" he asked.

She nodded. "But I've never parachuted."

"You won't need to parachute. We'll skim across the surface and then lift up a few feet, staying over the water the whole time. If something happens to the plane, you can jump out and swim with the fish."

Kim took a deep breath, her palms sweaty and her nerves zinging. "I'm ready."

The propeller on the front of his brother's small single-engine seaplane spun around, picking up speed, and her heart beat faster and faster.

You can do this, she told herself. *You* have *to do this.*

As they moved forward, the high squeal ringing in her ears dropped to a low buzz. Out her side window a white wake followed the slender float as it cut through the water.

"Okay?" Nathaniel asked, glancing her way as he worked the controls.

"Yes." She held tight to her seatbelt and gritted her teeth as the plane lifted higher. "I'm . . . okay."

And she really was.

Youngs Bay stretched out before them, and she giggled with nervous relief, giddy as Theresa on too much sugar.

"This is amazing," she said, her voice soaring an octave higher than normal.

Nathaniel laughed as if energized by her excitement. "There are many lakes in Sweden. My brother and I have been flying float planes since we were in high school even if our mother didn't want us to."

"Was she afraid you'd get hurt?" she asked.

He shook his head. "She was more afraid for the plane. It wasn't ours, but a neighbor's."

Kim urged Nathaniel to go a little higher and marveled at the scene below, images she never would have seen with her own eyes if she hadn't agreed to fly.

She thought of her mother and the risk involved. Since the crash, Kim had avoided all kinds of risk. She had even avoided risk in her relationships by keeping tight control over her emotions.

Until Nathaniel.

"Thank you," she said, touching his shoulder.

He grinned. "No, my dear Kimberly, thank *you*."

EARLY THE NEXT morning, Kim checked on the little blackbird by the side door in the party room. She'd placed leaves and birdseed in the box with it, along with a bowl of water. The song by the Beatles came to mind, as she checked its broken wing and urged it to fly. Instead, it fluttered around, hobbling, with only little jumps here and there.

"What are we going to do when its wing heals and we have a bird flying around the shop?" Rachel asked, coming up behind her.

Kim shrugged. "I'll open the door and let it go."

She heard her name and looked through the connecting door into the main room of the shop, where Meredith was talking on the phone.

"Sorry," Meredith said with a conniving note in her voice. "She's not available right now."

Kim walked toward her. "Is that for me?"

Meredith glanced at her and grimaced. "Well, she might be here after all. Hold on."

Kim narrowed her gaze on the girl and took the phone away from her. "Why didn't you call me over?"

"You want me calling out across the shop?" Meredith asked, her hands on her hips.

"If the phone call is for me," Kim said, "then, *yes!*"

Meredith rolled her eyes and walked away in a huff.

"Hello?" Kim greeted the person on the other end of the line, hoping it was Nathaniel.

It wasn't. It was one of her friends from the Portland art show.

"Kim, I've been talking to the others, and we really need to know if you plan to open the gallery with us. Mark, Ellie, and I are looking at possible locations, and as soon as we find one, we'll need the money for the first month's rent."

She hesitated, then glanced toward Andi and Rachel, who were filling the display case with fresh cupcakes. "Can I give you an answer by the end of the week?"

"Sure, Kim, but the sooner you decide, the better. We need you."

Kim hung up, confident that by the end of the week, she'd know if there would still be a cupcake shop to stand in her way or if the choice would be a no-brainer.

At least she had options. If Creative Cupcakes closed down, she didn't know what Andi and Rachel would do.

Through the large front window she caught sight of a motorcycle and ran forward—except it wasn't Nathaniel's blue Honda Shadow but a black Harley-Davidson.

"Andi! Rachel! You have to see this," Kim called as she headed for the door. "I think Guy Armstrong got his license back."

Kim remembered Guy telling them he'd never drive again after his DUI ten years before. That's why he rode to work each day on his bicycle. Guess he changed his mind.

Andi and Rachel followed her outside to the curb, where Guy pulled an old black helmet off his head.

"What do you think?" he asked, pride making him puff out his chest like a prizefighter.

"Very nice!" Rachel exclaimed.

Andi agreed. "Looks great."

"Took a few hundred dollars to fix, but after seeing Kim's friend on his bike the other day, I decided to go for it."

Kim's gaze took in his short stature and pale white ponytailed head, and she frowned. "Where did you get the money?"

"I sold a few things," he told her and grinned, revealing his missing tooth, which gave him the appearance of a . . . troll.

Could Guy Armstrong be their cupcake thief?

A shriek sounded from within the shop, cutting into her thoughts and making her run back through the door behind Andi and Rachel.

"What's wrong?" Andi demanded.

Theresa cowered in the corner, her hands covering half her face. Instead of answering, she pointed to the end of the counter, her finger trembling.

Rachel gasped. "Where are the wedding cupcakes?"

"The cupcakes for Nathaniel's brother's wedding?" Kim asked. She froze, staring at the empty counter where they'd stacked the luscious white sponge cakes with toffee icing she'd decorated all morning. *"No!"*

"I didn't see anything," Meredith said, lifting her nose.

"That's because you were texting on your cell phone," Theresa accused.

"No," Meredith shot back. "It's because you were flirting with Eric."

"Meredith, we told you no cell phones while working," Andi said, walking toward her.

"Andi," Kim said, counting to ten before she spoke so she wouldn't scream, "the wedding is in two hours. What are we going to do?"

"The thief must have slipped into the shop and taken them out the side door while we were out front," Rachel said, and pursed her lips. "I wish the mailman would bring us the dye pack we ordered. The Cupcake Bandit has gone too far this time. We need the sales from this event to buy the building."

"I need the cupcakes," Kim exclaimed. "What am I supposed to tell Nathaniel and his family?"

"We'll bake a new batch," Andi said, pulling out a bowl from under the counter. "Quick! Everyone work together. With a little luck, we'll have them baked, iced, and decorated just in time."

HOWEVER, TIME DIDN'T seem to be on their side, not with Mr. Warden calling to tell them he'd found a buyer for the building if they couldn't purchase it themselves within the next three days. Andi and Kim's father's sudden appearance didn't help either.

"What's going on in here?" he demanded. "I've never seen such chaos."

Theresa bent down to clean the icing she'd spilled on the floor, but Eric rushed from the kitchen with a tray of hot cupcakes in his hands, didn't see the mess, and slipped. Andi's cry of warning came a second too late, but she did manage to save the cupcakes by lifting the ends of her apron and using it like a catcher's mitt.

Kim let out a sigh of relief. "Great play by Andi Burke."

Then, careful to use potholders, Kim retrieved the tray from her sister and took the cupcakes to her workstation where she'd been creating white wedding doves out of a combination of fondant and piped sugar frosting.

"We're under pressure," Andi told their father.

"What pressure?" he asked, furrowing his brow. "How hard can it be to bake cupcakes?"

"Dad!" Kim shouted, using a knife to ice a previous batch that had cooled. "*Please.*"

"Kim, I didn't mean you. I was talking to Andi. Everyone knows you always do your best."

"No, I don't," she shot back. "I make mistakes just like everybody else."

"Kim, stay out of this," her father warned.

"No, I will *not* stay out of it. I will not listen to you criticize Andi ever again. What we need right now, what we've needed ever since Mom died, is your support."

Her father stared at her as if he didn't recognize her. Then he turned and without another word went back out the door.

Andi stared at her, too. "Thanks, Kim."

Kim nodded and watched her sister limp toward the kitchen. "Wait! Andi, what's wrong with your foot?"

Andi cringed. "I think I sprained it while trying to save the cupcakes from hitting the floor."

RACHEL AND ANDI cracked eggs, measured flour, sugar, butter and baking powder, and dumped them into the big industrial mixer. Eric and Theresa poured the batter into the cupcake wrappers lining the molded trays and put them in the oven. And as soon as they cooled, Meredith and Kim went to work frosting and decorating. Heather manned the cupcake counter and kept Mia and Taylor out of the way.

"Ten minutes, Kim," Andi warned, looking at the clock.

"Finished," Kim called out as she packaged the last dozen wedding cupcakes into the open boxes.

Mike drove the Cupcake Mobile to the Riverview Community Park and Pavilion, and Kim was thankful they'd made it before the wedding ceremony started. She and Rachel jumped out and began to unload.

"You can put the cupcakes over there," a blond-haired, blue-eyed woman directed them. "My brother and his new wife will love these."

Kim remembered Nathaniel telling her his parents and younger sister were flying over from Sweden for the wedding and this young woman looked just like him.

"Are you Linnea?" Kim asked. "I'm a . . . friend of your brother, Nathaniel."

"More than a friend," he corrected, coming toward them and giving her shoulders a squeeze. "Kim is my date."

"I have to work," she reminded him with a smile.

"Only part of the evening," he said. "The other part you can spend with me."

"Nice to meet you," Linnea said, shaking her hand.

"Are you sure you'll be able to handle this by yourself?" Rachel asked, glancing around at all the people filling the gardens.

"Of course," Kim assured her. "Now that the cupcakes are here, all I have to do is serve them. You and Mike can leave."

"Call if you run into any problems," Rachel whispered, and taking Mike's arm, she headed back to the truck.

KIM WATCHED NATHANIEL's brother and his bride exchange marriage vows and imagined herself watching Andi and Jake's wedding in September and then Rachel and Mike's on Christmas Eve. Watching, always watching, always alone.

And with Nathaniel leaving in three days, she didn't have any prospects of changing her single status any more than she could force herself to board a commercial jet.

"Come with me," Nathaniel coaxed, his voice low as they shared a dance away from the crowd.

She tilted her head back to look up at him. "Where?"

"To Sweden. My family has a big estate. You can room with my sister. She'd love to visit with you."

"I can't."

"You *can*. I know you can. I have faith in you."

For one moment she imagined sitting beside Nathaniel on the plane and touring Sweden with her paint-brushes in her pocket, but she grew weak at the notion of being thousands of feet up in the air, with no control over her safety.

"Flying in the hot air balloon and flying in the low-flying seaplane with you helped, but I'm not ready to board a commercial airliner yet, especially one flying halfway around the world."

Nathaniel couldn't hide his disappointment. It showed through his eyes and was etched in every muscle on his face. "*Ja*, I know. It's too soon."

She loved the fact he didn't pressure her or argue with her, like Gavin. Her ex-boyfriend hadn't understood. Not like Nathaniel, who would be another ex, all because she wasn't brave enough to fly.

"I'm so sorry," she said, and hoped he realized how hard it was for her to say that, how hard it would be to let him go.

BEFORE THE TRADITIONAL cutting of the cake, or, in this case, the bride and groom feeding each other the cup-cakes, Kim circled around each table distributing cup-cakes to each guest's plate. Then she stood beside Caleb, the young man Jake had recommended from the local media crew to videotape the event.

Her pocket buzzed, and when she took out her cell phone to answer the call, she found her sister in hysterics.

"Andi, calm down and tell me what's wrong."

"I lost my diamond engagement ring. *It fell into the cupcake batter!*"

Kim glanced around at all the guests who each had a cupcake on their plate waiting to be eaten. "The batter for the second set of wedding cupcakes?"

"Yes!"

"Are you sure? Maybe you misplaced the ring, took it off while you were baking or to wash your hands?"

"We watched the security camera footage. Plain as day it shows me take off the food handler's gloves and the ring sliding off my finger and into the bowl of batter below."

"How could you let something like this happen?" Kim demanded.

"It was an accident!"

Kim took a deep breath. It was because of the Cupcake Bandit. If he hadn't stolen the cupcakes, they wouldn't have been in a rush. "What do you want me to do?"

"You have to *find* it."

"How am I supposed to do that?"

"Think of something, Kim. You can't let them eat those cupcakes. Mike, Rachel, and I are already on our way and will be there in three minutes. But if someone bites into the cupcake with the ring and breaks a tooth or swallows it and chokes, we could be facing a lawsuit." Andi let out a choked cry. "Oh, please don't let anyone swallow my ring. I might never get it back."

Kim hung up, but then her heart leaped into her chest as she saw that the bride and groom had each picked up a cupcake and were preparing to give each other a taste.

Should she signal Nathaniel?

There was no time. She had to do something, and she had to do it *now*.

"Stop!" she called across the crowd. "Don't eat the cupcakes!"

No one heard her. The crowd had gathered in tight and were cheering the couple on, hoping to see them smash the cupcakes into each other's mouths.

Kim ran forward and shouted again. She pushed her way between two obese women and shoved past a man who didn't want to wait for the bride and groom. He opened his mouth to take a bite of his cupcake, and Kim knew there would be no avoiding conflict this time.

Stepping close, she knocked the cupcake to the ground. Five more steps and she knocked the cupcakes away from the bride and groom. Then she ran toward every person in the vicinity who lifted a cupcake to their mouth.

Several people gasped, others screamed, and suddenly everyone was in an uproar.

"I'll sue you," the mother of the bride hollered, her face contorted with rage. "You won't see a penny of profit from this wedding. I'll sue Creative Cupcakes for everything they've got!"

The bride took a napkin and tried to wipe cake off her icing-covered dress. Then the bride looked up at her with horror-stricken eyes. "What have you done?"

"I'm sorry," Kim said, her throat aching with tension. "I tried to warn you, but you didn't hear, and then there was no time. My sister lost her ring in one of the cupcakes."

"What kind of catering company would do such thing?" Nathaniel's mother demanded in her heavy Swedish accent.

Kim shrank back from the accusations, and her gaze locked on Nathaniel's face, filled with as much shock as the bride and groom and the two mothers.

"No one eat the cupcakes," he ordered, moving through the crowd toward her.

"We'll make amends," Kim added.

"Make amends?" the bride asked. "You ruined my wedding!"

The bride must have realized Caleb was capturing every second of the chaos on his video camera, because she picked up another cupcake and smashed it straight into his lens.

Kim realized she hadn't found Andi's ring and ran from table to table smashing all the cupcakes with her hands, hoping to feel a piece of hard metal. After smashing over two dozen cupcakes, something poked the palm of her hand.

Pulling apart the remains of the traditional Swedish wedding cake, she pulled out the diamond ring and held it up.

"See?" she said, and looked at the bride. "This is my sister's engagement ring. Imagine if your ring had fallen into the batter. What would you have me do?"

"Leave," the bride's mother said, pointing a finger toward the parking lot.

Nathaniel took her elbow. "I'll take you home."

She nodded and headed toward his truck. His family would never welcome her now, never forgive her. Her stomach wrenched into fits of twisted agony. Would this change Nathaniel's opinion of her as well? She shot him a quick glance, but his expression didn't reveal an answer.

She opened the passenger side door, ready to climb in, and a doll fell out. *Mia's doll.*

Picking the toy off the ground, she held it up and stared at him. "How did Mia's doll get in your truck?"

Nathaniel's eyes widened. "I have no idea."

Could Nathaniel be the Cupcake Bandit? Her mind raced to place him at the scene of every disappearance. He'd been at the fire. He'd been at the festival. The thief had not switched the doll for the cupcakes at the Astoria Column. Maybe because Nathaniel had been with her?

The security camera had caught sight of someone with pale hair, and Nathaniel's hair was blond. One of the women at the Scandinavian Festival had described the troll handing out cupcakes as "tall" and "handsome." Of course, the little old lady had been rather short, so many people could be tall from her point of view, and who knew what type of man she thought handsome.

"I've never seen that doll before," Nathaniel told her.

Kim wasn't sure she could believe him. Instead, she feared that while Andi and Rachel had found true love, she'd lost her heart to a cupcake thief.

A loud, familiar clanking sound could be heard coming around the corner, and when the Cupcake Mobile parked, Andi, Rachel, and Mike jumped out.

"Did you find it?" Andi asked, her face lined with worry. Kim held up the ring. "Yes."

"You are not welcome here," the mother of the bride yelled, running toward them. "Go away!"

Andi, Rachel, and Mike glanced at each other, their mouths hanging open, as if not knowing what to do.

"Kim," Rachel called, holding open the Cupcake Mobile door. "Are you coming?"

Kim hesitated, looked at Nathaniel for one agonizing moment, and then ran toward them with both the ring and the doll in her hands.

"What happened?" Rachel asked, her eyes wide.

"Andi told me to stop them from eating the cupcakes, and so I—I smashed them. Now the bride's family is threatening to sue."

"*Sue?*" Rachel screeched. "Couldn't you find the ring without smashing the cupcakes? Why do you always do what Andi tells you?"

"I didn't mean for you to ruin the wedding or cause a scene," Andi said, taking the ring from her and slipping it back on her finger. "If they sue, they'll shut down our shop."

"It gets worse," Kim said, her stomach squeezing tight.

"How could it be worse?" Mike asked, rounding a turn in the road.

"They've refused to pay us for the wedding cupcakes."

"We won't be able to buy the building without the profits from this event," Rachel cried, turning around in her seat and bracing her hand on the dashboard. "Creative Cupcakes will be finished."

"Maybe that's what Kim planned all along," Andi said, a harsh edge entering her voice.

Kim stared at her. "What do you mean?"

"While you were smashing cupcakes," Rachel informed her, "one of your friends called the shop and said they'd rented a space in town to open your art gallery. When were you going to tell us? After Creative Cupcakes closed?"

"I didn't tell you because I knew you wouldn't want me to leave," Kim said, glancing around at each of them as they arrived at the cupcake shop.

"You'd abandon us for an art gallery?" Andi opened her door and climbed out. "Is that why you haven't been a team player this month?"

"I've always been a team player," Kim said, her throat burning as she followed them on to the sidewalk. "From day one I've worked long hours and backed you one hundred percent. But did you ever ask me what I wanted? No, you just assumed you could drag me into business with you. But the cupcake shop wasn't my idea. It wasn't *my* dream."

"Did you sabotage Creative Cupcakes on purpose?" Rachel asked, pointing to the doll in her hand. "Are *you* the Cupcake Bandit?"

"No."

"Then where did you find Mia's doll?" Andi demanded.

Kim cringed, wishing she were anywhere but here at this moment. "In Nathaniel's truck."

Their father had always condemned a show of emotion, especially when their mother died. Emotion was weak. That's why he thought Andi was weak. Andi always gave in to her emotions, but not her. She kept her feelings under control.

But she couldn't control the stinging in her eyes, or the tightness in her chest, or the widening hole in her stomach now.

Turning tail, she ran outside, stepped into the bushes . . . and puked.

Chapter Nine

Seize the moment. Remember all those women
on the *Titanic* who waved off the dessert cart.

—Erma Bombeck

KIM CRIED. SHE cried for her mother. Cried for the loss
of her dreams to travel the world. Cried over Andi's and
Rachel's accusations. Cried over Gavin, whom she never
really loved, and over the loss of Nathaniel, whom she
feared she did.

And she cried when she lifted the little blackbird into
the air, and it flapped its healed wing and flew off into the
early morning sky.

"Goodbye," she whispered. "I'll never forget you."

"And we'll never forget you."

Kim spun around and saw Andi and Rachel standing behind her, no longer angry, but smiling.

"You were right, Kim," Andi said, wrapping her arms around her. "I was so desperate to make my dream of a successful cupcake business come true that I didn't realize you may have had a different dream. Rachel and I never *asked* if you wanted to go into business with us. And if you want to leave, then . . . we have to let you go."

Rachel came forward to wrap her arms around her as well. "We have to let you make your own decisions."

"Thank you," Kim whispered.

"We've decided to hold a 'Save the Shop' sale tomorrow to sell off whatever we can to raise money to buy the building," Andi told her.

"I'll help," Kim offered. "I never meant to harm Creative Cupcakes' reputation."

Pop!

Kim darted with Rachel and Andi from the party room into the main shop hoping they'd finally caught their thief. Guy had helped them install the radio-transmitted dye pack under the cupcake a few hours earlier.

"Grandpa Lewy!" Rachel exclaimed.

The old man stood by the front door with his arms, chest, and face splattered with red dye and frosting. In his hands were what looked like the remains of an Oreo brownie cupcake.

Andi laughed. "Grandpa Lewy is the Cupcake Bandit?"

Kim laughed, too. Like Nathaniel, Grandpa Lewy had also been at the cupcake shop every time there had been a theft. His white hair was pale, and older women like Bernice considered him handsome. And the assisted living center where he lived was located between the community park where Nathaniel's brother got married and Nathaniel's private property. It would have been easy for him to have dropped Mia's doll into his truck if a door or window was open.

And if Grandpa Lewy was the cupcake thief, then that meant that Nathaniel was *not*.

"Grandpa," Rachel scolded, her face flushed, "why did you steal our cupcakes?"

"I didn't steal. You said I could have one any time."

"Why did you steal Mia's doll?" Andi asked.

The old man shook his head as if confused. "I found a doll. It looked familiar, so I put it in that thing that holds my memories."

"Your memory box?" Rachel prompted. "Is that where you hid all the cupcakes?"

"I don't know," he said, his eyes lacking focus.

"You wrote a ransom note in the Cupcake Diary," Kim said, handing him a towel to wipe his face.

"Your poster said you'd give a cupcake to anyone who found a doll," Grandpa Lewy said and frowned. "I found a doll, and I like cupcakes."

"But you didn't show up at the Astoria Column," Kim pointed out.

"I forgot." He wiped his face and stared at the smeared ink and icing on the white towel.

The phone rang, and Andi went around the counter to answer it. "Rachel," she said, holding the phone away from her ear, "the assisted living center says we need to bring your grandfather back right away. There's been an incident they need to discuss with us."

"What kind of incident?" Rachel asked, gripping her grandfather's arm.

Kim smiled. "Maybe they found the cupcakes."

The nurses were not happy campers. Kim didn't know who was worse—them or the bride's mother at the wedding.

"Do you see these boxes?" one nurse exclaimed, holding up a pink box with the Creative Cupcakes logo. "Last night we found half the residents on a sugar high that had them bouncing around like kids on a bouncy ball."

"The first batch of cupcakes for the wedding," Kim mused.

"Grandpa, did you have a cupcake party?" Rachel asked.

He wavered on his feet, and Rachel reached out to steady him.

"I made lots of friends," he told her and smiled, as if loopy. "They helped carry some of the boxes."

Kim frowned. "Rachel, I don't think he's feeling good."

"He looks pale," said the head nurse. "Let's sit him down."

However, before he could sit, Grandpa Lewy collapsed, and they had to call the hospital for an ambulance.

"HE'S OKAY," RACHEL assured them, returning to the shop a few hours later. "They hooked him up with an IV and are running tests."

"Maybe you should take him a triple-chocolate cupcake to cheer him up," Andi teased. "Might make him feel better."

"He didn't know what he was doing," Rachel said, shaking her head.

"It's okay," Kim assured her. "We can't blame him for loving our cupcakes."

"No, we can't blame *anyone*," Andi agreed and nodded toward the door. "Looks like you have a special delivery, Kim."

Kim turned and met Nathaniel's troubled, blue-eyed gaze.

"I came to say I'm sorry about last night," he said, handing her a large bouquet of bright red, heavenly scented roses. "I promise you, I didn't take the doll or any of the cupcakes. I'm not your thief."

"We know," Rachel assured him. "It was my grandfather."

"I'm sorry I ruined your brother's wedding," Kim told him.

Nathaniel smiled. "You didn't ruin it, you made it memorable. After you left, my brother and his bride looked at each other, realized their love for each other had nothing to do with cupcakes, and started laughing."

"They aren't going to sue?" Andi asked, her face filled with hope.

"No one is going to sue," he assured them and set a piece of paper on the counter. "And here is a check to cover the cost of the cupcakes."

Kim shook her head. "We can't accept this—not after what I did."

"The money is to help save the shop," Nathaniel told them. "My new sister-in-law agrees with you. She would have smashed cupcakes herself if she'd lost *her* ring in the batter. But you didn't smash all of them. There were plenty of cupcakes left for everyone to enjoy."

"Thank you," Andi said, taking the check. "But I'm afraid we're going to need a lot more than this to buy the building."

"Every bit helps, *ja?*" he asked.

Kim nodded, and Nathaniel took both her hands and squeezed her fingers. "I also came to say goodbye."

Kim was afraid of that. "I'll miss you."

"I'll miss you, too. Are you sure you don't want to come?"

"I would if I could," Kim assured him. "But I—I can't."

"I'll call you," he promised.

Kim nodded, her stomach so tight she wondered if she'd have to make another trip to the bushes. "Send me a postcard."

He looked at her with an expression so intense she could barely breathe. "Goodbye, Kimberly."

Her eyes stung, and her entire body went rigid with dread at the thought of being left behind again. *Please don't go.* She wanted to scream the words at the top of her lungs but didn't. How could she? What right did she have to even ask? She couldn't tie him down like his previous girlfriend had tried to do.

He couldn't stay. And she couldn't go. Once again, it

seemed history was repeating itself, only with different players.

"Goodbye," she said, her voice choked, and then, all at once she flung herself into his arms, pressed her body to his, and squeezed him as hard as she could.

His arms wrapped around her, and his head dropped down over her shoulder, as if the moment was killing him, too. Then he released her, gave her a parting grin . . . and was gone.

THE SPECIAL "SAVE the Shop" sale brought in a crowd. Kim suspected that Jake's newspaper story in the *Astoria Sun* titled "Identity of Cupcake Bandit Revealed: Grandpa with Alzheimer's Has Craving for Cupcakes" had something to do with it.

Andi and Jake decided to forgo their honeymoon and sell the Hawaii vacation tickets they'd coveted for so long.

"I'll get to Hawaii someday," Andi said, her face full of determination. "But buying the building to save Creative Cupcakes is more important."

Rachel put her jewelry box into the auction, swung her red curls over her shoulder, and told them, "Looks aren't everything."

Andi gasped. "I can't believe you, of all people, said that, Miss I Won't Leave the House without My Makeup."

"Mike tells me I'm beautiful every day," Rachel assured her. "That's all I need."

Mike had offered to sell off a prized miniature set

model he'd worked on for a canceled TV series, and Kim decided to auction off all the paintings adorning the walls of the cupcake shop.

"Won't you need them to open the art gallery with your friends?" Andi asked.

"I've found I like decorating cupcakes as much as I like painting," she told her. "And by staying with Creative Cupcakes, I can do both. Besides, we're a *team*." She glanced at Meredith and narrowed her eyes. "Except for that one."

Walking over to the hawk-eyed, teenage redhead, she arched a brow and announced, "Meredith, you're fired."

The girl scrunched up her nose in disgust. "You can't fire me. Andi, tell her how valuable I am."

Andi shook her head. "Kim is co-owner of this shop, and if she says you're fired, then you're fired."

"But—"

"No buts," Andi continued. "Kim has a right to make her own decisions."

"So do I," Guy said. He walked over to Andi and handed her a check for $20,000. "I decided I don't need a Harley after all. My wild days on the motorcycle are behind me, and it's never helped me pick up chicks."

The Romance Writers group who met in the shop on Tuesdays also brought in a donation, as did the parents of all the children involved in the kids' cupcake camp that Andi had started as an afternoon program. The dateless women who commiserated with each other at the Saturday Night Cupcake Club and friends from the local police station also gave money.

"Can't have our favorite cupcake shop go out of business," Officer Ian Lockwell told them.

"No, we can't," William Burke agreed.

Kim jumped back with a jolt of surprise. She hadn't seen her father drift in with the crowd.

"Dad!" Andi exclaimed. "What are you doing here?"

Kim watched her father fiddle with his wallet, turning it over in his hand, while looking around at the shop filled with people.

Finally, he cleared his throat and looked right at her, his eyes moist. "Your mother loved to dream. *My* dream was to keep you all safe, even if that meant talking you out of things you wanted to do from time to time. I tried to steer you toward what I thought was best. I was wrong when I tried to discourage you from opening the cupcake shop. You've worked hard for this, and . . . I'm proud of you." He shifted his gaze to Andi. "I'm proud of *all* of you."

"So am I," Rachel's mother said, drawing near. "You've all inspired me to pursue my own dream. Since I took out the old Singer sewing machine to alter Rachel's wedding dress, I decided I liked it so much I want to open a bridal shop!"

"That's wonderful," Andi said, her voice excited. "Maybe you can work on my wedding dress, too."

"And mine," Kim said and blushed. "I didn't mean a wedding dress for me, but a bridesmaid dress. I'll need two of them, one for each wedding."

Kim thought she saw a glimmer of warmth pass through her father's eyes as he looked at Rachel's mom. But Sarah Donovan locked her gaze on Guy, who stepped forward, took her hand, and drew her away with a bigger grin on his face than Kim had ever seen.

"Do you have enough money to buy the shop?" Kim's father asked, turning his attention back to them.

Kim looked at Andi, who hesitated, then shook her head.

"We're still short."

"I'll make up the difference," he told them, "and you can repay me when you can."

Kim looked at her sister. "We can buy the building!"

"I—I don't know what to say, Dad," Andi said, tears welling in her eyes. "Except—thank you."

He took a step closer and draped an arm across each of their shoulders in what Kim thought he meant as a hug. This was a huge step for a man who had nearly strained their relationship beyond repair.

"Yes," Kim said and kissed his cheek. "Thank you."

"Dream big," he told them. "And make Creative Cupcakes a success."

AFTER SIGNING THE papers transferring ownership of the building into their names the following morning, Kim, Andi, and Rachel took one of their biggest chocolate chip cupcakes with chocolate butter cream frosting to the hospital for Grandpa Lewy.

"The doctors said they may have misdiagnosed your grandfather," Bernice told them, her hand intertwined with Rachel's grandfather's. "He has a severe bladder infection, which often produces the same characteristics of

Alzheimer's. They say it must have been building in his system for several months."

Rachel's mouth popped open. "Do you mean he can get better?"

"What do you mean, 'get better'?" he asked. "What's wrong with me now?"

"You've been hiding our cupcakes in your memory box and taking them out of our store," Rachel told him. "We lost a lot of money."

Grandpa Lewy opened the memory box covered with photos of Rachel and her parents, and some older ones of the time he spent as a young man with Bernice. "You mean this money?"

Everyone in the room drew in their breath as they all stared at the assortment of fives, tens, and twenties.

"I didn't eat all of the cupcakes," Grandpa Lewy said and chuckled. "I sold some for you at the festival and at the center. The nurses there won't let us have any sweets. I knew if the head nurse caught me, I'd be in trouble, but . . . the sweetest things in life are worth the risk."

His words pierced Kim's heart, and she thought of Nathaniel. He was probably already at the airport, waiting to board his plane, which would leave in three hours.

"Grandpa Lewy is right," Kim said, her heart leaping. "Sometimes the sweetest things *are* worth a little risk."

As if reading her mind, Rachel asked, "How many roses did Nathaniel bring you in that last bouquet?"

"Thirty-six."

"That means, '*I will remember our romantic moments,*'" Rachel interpreted.

"I don't want to just remember them," Kim said. "I want to *live* them."

"Do you need a ride to the airport?" Andi asked, a smile hovering on the edge of her lips.

Kim thought her insides would cave in and collapse into a muddled heap at the bottom of her stomach. "I gave all the money I'd saved for the art gallery and all the profits from my paintings to help buy the building for Creative Cupcakes. I don't have money for a ticket."

"Use *this*," Rachel said, handing her the money from Grandpa Lewy's memory box.

"Are you sure?" Kim asked, staring at what looked to be close to $2,000.

"The cupcake shop is safe, thanks to your contributions," Andi told her. "Do you have your passport?"

All at once the world seemed to spin, leaving her breathless and excited all at the same time.

"Yes, my passport is always with me, always in my pocket next to my wings pin," she said, pulling it out and flapping the booklet in the air. "Ready to fly!"

Chapter Ten

Real love stories never have endings.

—**Richard Bach**

"How can I get to the airport in time?" Kim asked, as they stood by the waterfront outside the Astoria hospital. She closed her cell phone. "The cab company says they can't get here for another fifteen minutes."

Andi shook her head. "Jake's busy working at the office, and he took my car."

"Mike's meeting a movie producer interested in hiring him to build set models," Rachel added. "He said he wouldn't be able to pick us back up for another hour, and my mother's car is in the repair shop."

"And I don't have a car," Kim said, searching her brain for an answer.

"We have the Cupcake Mobile," Andi suggested.

"But you can't drive with your sprained foot, and Rachel and I can't drive a stick shift," Kim told her. "What about our new recruits? Aren't any of them at the shop?"

Andi shook her head. "Only Heather, who is babysitting Mia and Taylor, and she doesn't have her driver's license."

"What about Guy?" Rachel suggested. "He just got his license back, and he's the one who sold us the Cupcake Mobile in the first place."

Kim punched his number into her cell phone. "Guy, if you aren't in the middle of giving someone a tattoo I could really use your help."

FIVE MINUTES LATER the Cupcake Mobile rattled around the corner to pick them up.

"No problems?" Kim asked. "Heather found the keys?"

Guy hesitated. "Yeah, but I have to warn you. I haven't driven an enclosed vehicle in over twenty years. I may be a little rusty."

Rusty was an understatement. The Cupcake Mobile lurched forward and backward every time Guy had to shift or use the clutch. Kim gripped the seat in front of her on either side, squeezed her eyes shut, and took a deep breath. Flying couldn't be any harder than surviving this ride.

Glancing at her watch, she marked another minute had passed since the last time she looked at it.

"Can't this truck go any faster?" she asked.

"Sorry," Guy told her. "The thing's an antique. She can only handle fifty-five miles an hour without falling apart."

After a two-hour ride, the clinking, clattering Cupcake Mobile pulled up to the drop-off curb with only forty-five minutes to spare.

"They could already be boarding," Rachel warned. "Andi, how are you doing with that foot?"

"It hurts, but I can hobble," Andi said, limping behind them through the airport entrance.

Kim got in line at the ticket counter, murmuring, "Faith can move mountains. Faith can move mountains. Faith can move mountains."

Right now she'd be happy if it just moved this line in front of her. What if she couldn't get her ticket in time? How long before the next flight? Would she have to fly alone?

She'd tried to call Nathaniel on his cell phone several times but got no answer. On her fourth try, his brother picked up and said Nathaniel had left the phone with him.

"Inconceivable!" Rachel exclaimed. "Who can travel without a phone?"

"Someone who isn't expecting any calls," Andi said and shuffled forward as the people in front of them finally parted.

"I need a ticket to Göteborg, Sweden, with a stopover flight in Amsterdam, leaving at three o'clock," Kim said, leaning over the counter. "Can you tell me if passenger Nathaniel Sjölander has checked in for that flight?"

"Yes, he's checked in," the ticket lady confirmed after checking.

Rachel gasped. "Kim's going to need clothes, toiletries, and makeup."

Andi agreed. "You go that way, and I'll go the other, and we'll all meet up at the security gate."

Kim counted the seconds as Rachel and Andi split up in search of supplies from the airport shops lining the corridor.

"I don't believe we have any seats left," the ticket agent said, searching the computer screen in front of her. "Wait. Here's one. Do you have any luggage?"

"No," Kim said.

The woman leaned her head around the counter to look at her. "No carry-on bag?"

"Please," Kim said, handing the agent her passport and wishing the woman would hurry. "Just the ticket."

"I'll call ahead and tell them to hold the plane," the woman told her. "But if you don't hurry, they'll close the door."

Kim ran toward the security gate, ticket in hand with only thirty minutes to go ... and skidded to a stop in front of Nathaniel, who was on his way back out.

He gave her an incredulous look. "Kimberly, what are you doing here?"

Kim longed to fling herself into his arms, gaze into his eyes, kiss him, and tell him how just standing beside him made her heart skip right off the charts. But there would be plenty of time for that later, once they were in Sweden and the clock was no longer an issue.

For now, she simply held up her ticket. "I decided I couldn't stay and let you leave me behind."

His blue eyes sparkled, and his mouth curved into a wide grin. "I decided I couldn't go if you weren't coming with me."

Kim gasped. "Really?"

"Really." Nathaniel drew her close and kissed her lips, his breath warm against her cheek. When he pulled back, his eyes were lit with mischief. "Ready for a taste of adventure?"

Kim felt as if her happiness would explode inside her if she didn't smile and let at least some of it out. "Actually, I think I'm ready for a taste of romance."

"I think I can remedy that," he assured her.

With a clap of running feet, Andi and Rachel both ran toward them from opposite directions.

Andi reached her first. "Here's a backpack, an Oregon Ducks sweatshirt—because Sweden is cold—a travel toothbrush, and a candy bag of red Swedish fish."

"I bought you perfume, lipstick, a CD player, and a *Rosetta Stone* translator program," Rachel told her. "You can learn the language on the plane."

Nathaniel laughed. "We do speak English."

Kim gave both her sister and Rachel a big hug. "Take care of Creative Cupcakes until I get back," she told them.

"We'll keep up with our notes in the Cupcake Diary via email," Andi promised. "But remember you'll have to come back for my wedding in September."

Rachel nodded. "And mine at Christmas."

"No need to worry," Nathaniel told them. "I only planned to stay in Sweden a month."

"A month?" Kim asked. "You said if your mother had her way, you'd stay there forever."

Nathaniel grinned. "If my mother had her way, *ja*. But I make my own decisions, and my home is now in Astoria. Still want to come with me?"

"Yes," Kim said, and taking his hand, she started to move through the security line toward the fulfillment of her dreams.

"Wait! I almost forgot!" Running up to the gate, Andi gave her one last item—the one thing that meant as much to her as her passport.

A paintbrush.

Recipe for
COCONUT MACAROON CUPCAKES

From Patty Emmert of Port Orchard, Washington

3 cups coconut
⅔ cup sugar
1 egg white
6 Tbsp. cake flour
½ tsp. baking powder
½ tsp. almond extract
1 egg white
Candied cherries

Combine coconut, ⅓ cup sugar, and 1 egg white in a double boiler. Cook over boiling water until hot, stirring occasionally. Remove from heat.

Sift flour and baking powder together. Add to coconut mixture.

Add almond extract. Mix well.

Beat the other egg white in a separate bowl until foamy. Add remaining sugar gradually, 2 teaspoons at a time. Continue beating until the mixture will stand in soft peaks. Fold into the coconut mixture.

Place paper liners into 8 muffin pans and fill with batter. Top with cherries.

Bake in a slow oven (325°) for about 25 minutes.

Makes 8.

*Keep reading for excerpts from the first two
books in* The Cupcake Diaries *series,*

SWEET ON YOU

and

RECIPE FOR LOVE

now available from Avon Impulse.

An Excerpt from

THE CUPCAKE DIARIES: SWEET ON YOU

Forget love . . . I'd rather fall in chocolate!

—Author unknown

ANDI CAST A glance over the rowdy karaoke crowd to the man sitting at the front table with the clear plastic bakery box in his possession.

"What am I supposed to say?" she whispered, looking back at her sister, Kim, and their friend Rachel as the three of them huddled together. "Can I have your cupcake? He'll think I'm a lunatic."

"Say 'please,' and tell him about our tradition," Kim suggested.

"Offer him money." Rachel dug through her dilapidated Gucci knockoff purse and withdrew a ten-dollar bill. "And let him know we're celebrating your sister's birthday."

"You did promise me a cupcake for my birthday," Kim said with an impish grin. "Besides, the guy doesn't look like he plans to eat it. He hasn't even glanced at the cupcake since the old woman came in and delivered the box."

Andi tucked a loose strand of her dark blond hair behind her ear and drew in a deep breath. She wasn't used to taking food from anyone. Usually she was on the other end—giving it away. Her fault. She didn't plan ahead.

Why couldn't any of the businesses here be open twenty-four hours like in Portland? Out of the two dozen eclectic cafes and restaurants along the Astoria waterfront promising to satisfy customers' palates, shouldn't at least one cater to late-night customers like herself? No, they all shut down at 10:30, some earlier, as if they knew she was coming. That's what she got for living in a small town. Anticipation but no cake.

However, she was determined not to let her younger sister down. She'd promised Kim a cupcake for her twenty-sixth birthday, and she'd try her best to procure one, even if it meant making a fool of herself.

Andi shot her ever-popular friend Rachel a wry look. "You know you're better at this than I am."

Rachel grinned. "You're going to have to start interacting with the opposite sex again sometime."

Maybe. But not on the personal level, Rachel's tone suggested. Andi's divorce the previous year had left behind a bitter aftertaste no amount of sweet talk could dissolve.

Pushing back her chair, she stood up. "Tonight, all I want is the cupcake."

ANDI HAD TAKEN only a few steps when the man with the bakery box turned his head and smiled.

He probably thought she was coming over, hoping to find a date. Why shouldn't he? The Captain's Port was filled with people looking for a connection, if not for a lifetime, then at least for the hour or so they shared within the friendly confines of the restaurant's casual, communal atmosphere.

She hesitated midstep before continuing forward. Heat rushed into her cheeks. Dressed in jeans and a navy blue tie and sport jacket, he was even better looking than she'd first thought. Thirtyish. Light brown hair, fair skin with an evening shadow along his jaw, and the most amazing gold-flecked, chocolate brown eyes she'd ever seen. *Oh my.* He could have his pick of any woman in the place. Any woman in Astoria, Oregon.

"Hi," he said.

Andi swallowed the nervous tension gathering at the back of her throat and managed a smile in return. "Hi. I'm sorry to bother you, but it's my sister's birthday, and I promised her a cupcake." She nodded toward the see-through box and waved the ten-dollar bill. "Is there any chance I can persuade you to sell the one you have here?"

His brows shot up. "You want my cupcake?"

"I meant to bake a batch this afternoon," she gushed, her words tumbling over themselves, "but I ended up packing spring break lunches for the needy kids in the school district. Have you heard of the Kids' Coalition backpack program?"

He nodded. "Yes, I think the *Astoria Sun* featured the free lunch backpack program on the community page a few weeks ago."

"I'm a volunteer," she explained. "And after I finished, I tried to buy a cupcake but didn't get to the store in time. I've never let my sister down before, and I feel awful."

The new addition to her list of top ten dream-worthy males leaned back in his chair and pressed his lips together, as if considering her request, then shook his head. "I'd love to help you, but—"

"Please." Andi gasped, appalled she'd stooped to begging. She straightened her shoulders and lifted her chin. "I understand if you can't, it's just that my sister, Kim, my friend Rachel, and I have a tradition."

"What kind of tradition?"

Andi pointed to their table, and Kim and Rachel smiled and waved. "Our birthdays are spaced four months apart, so we split a celebration cupcake three ways and set new goals for ourselves from one person's birthday to the next. It's easier than trying to set goals for an entire year."

"I don't suppose you could set your goals without the cupcake?" he asked, his eyes sparkling with amusement.

Andi smiled. "It wouldn't be the same."

"If the cupcake were mine to give, it would be yours. But this particular cupcake was delivered for a research project I have at work."

"Wish I had your job." Andi dropped into the chair he pulled out for her and placed her hands flat on the table. "What if I told you it's been a really tough day, tough week, tough year?"

He pushed his empty coffee cup aside, and the corners of his mouth twitched upward. "I'd say I could argue the same."

"But did you spend the last three hours running all over town looking for a cupcake?" she challenged, playfully mimicking Rachel's flirtatious, sing-song tone. "The Pig 'n Pancake was closed, along with the supermarket, and the cafe down the street said they don't even sell them anymore. And then . . . I met you."

He covered her left hand with his own, and although the unexpected contact made her jump, she ignored the impulse to pull her fingers away. His gesture seemed more an act of compassion than anything else, and, frankly, she liked the feel of his firm yet gentle touch.

"What if I told you," he said, leaning forward, "that I've traveled five hundred and seventy miles and waited sixty-three days to taste this one cupcake?"

Andi leaned toward him as well. "I'd say that's ridiculous. There's no cupcake in Astoria worth all that trouble."

"What if this particular cupcake isn't from Astoria?"

"No?" She took another look at the box but didn't see a label. "Where's it from?"

"Hollande's French Pastry Parlor outside of Portland."

"What if I told you I would send you a dozen Hollande's cupcakes tomorrow?"

"What if I told *you*," he said, and stopped to release a deep, throaty chuckle, "this is the last morsel of food I have to eat before I starve to death today?"

Andi laughed. "I'd say that's a good way to go. Or I could invite you to my place and cook you dinner."

Her heart stopped, stunned by her own words, then rebooted a moment later when their gazes locked, and he smiled at her.

"You can have the cupcake on one condition."

"Which is?"

Giving her a wink, he slid the bakery box toward her. Then he leaned his head in close and whispered in her ear.

An Excerpt from

THE CUPCAKE DIARIES: RECIPE FOR LOVE

Life is uncertain. Eat dessert first.

—Ernestine Ulmer

RACHEL PUSHED THROUGH the double doors of the kitchen, took one look at the masked man at the counter, and dropped the freshly baked tray of cupcakes on the floor.

Did he plan to rob Creative Cupcakes, demand she hand over the money from the cash register? Her eyes darted around the frilly pink-and-white shop. The loud clang of the metal bakery pan hitting the tile had caused several customers sitting at the tables to glance in her direction. Would the masked man threaten the other people as well? How could she protect them?

She stepped over the white-frosted chocolate mess by her feet, tried to judge the distance to the telephone on the wall, and turned her attention back to the masked man before her. Maybe he wasn't a robber but someone dressed for a costume party or play. The man with the black masquerade mask covering the upper half of his face also wore a black cape.

"If this is a holdup, you picked the wrong place, Zorro." She tossed her fiery red curls over her shoulder with false bravado and laid a protective hand across the old bell-ringing register. "We don't have any money."

His hazel eyes gleamed through the holes in the mask, and he flashed her a disarming smile. "Maybe I can help with that."

He turned his hand to show an empty palm, and relief flooded over her. No gun. Then he closed his fingers and swung his fist around in the air three times. When he opened his palm again, he held a quarter, which he tossed in her direction.

Rachel caught the coin and laughed. "You're a magician."

"Mike the Magnificent," he said, extending his cape wide with one arm and taking a bow. "I'm here for the Lockwell party."

Rachel pointed to the door leading to the back party room. The space had originally been a tattoo shop, but the tattoo artist relocated to the rental next door. "The Lockwells aren't here yet. The party doesn't start until three."

"I came early to set up before the kids arrive," Mike told her. "Can't have them discovering my secrets."

"No, I guess not," Rachel agreed. "If they did, Mike the magician might not be so magnificent."

"Magnificence is hard to maintain." His lips twitched, as if suppressing a grin. "Are you Andi?"

She shook her head. "Rachel, Creative Cupcakes' stupendous co-owner, baker, and promoter."

This time a grin did escape his mouth, which led her to notice his strong, masculine jawline.

"Tell me, Rachel, what is it that makes you so stupendous?"

She gave him her most flirtatious smile. "Sorry, I can't reveal my secrets either."

"Afraid if I found out the truth, I might not think you're so impressively great?"

Rachel froze, fearing Mike the magician might be a mind reader as well. Careful to keep her smile intact, she forced herself to laugh off his comment.

"I just don't think it's nice to brag," she responded playfully.

"Chicken," he taunted in an equally playful tone as he made his way toward the party room door.

Despite the uneasy feeling he'd discovered more about her in three minutes than most men did in three years, she wished he'd stayed to chat a few minutes more.

Andi Burke, wearing one of the new, hot-pink Creative Cupcakes bibbed aprons, came in from the kitchen and stared at the cupcake mess on the floor. "What happened here?"

"Zorro came in, gave me a panic attack, and the tray slipped out of my hands." Rachel grabbed a couple of paper towels and squatted down to scoop up the crumpled cake and splattered frosting before her OCD kitchen safety friend could comment further. "Don't worry, I'll take care of the mess."

"I should have told you Officer Lockwell hired a magician for his daughter's birthday party." Andi bent to help her, and when they stood back up, she asked, "Did you speak to Mike?"

Rachel nodded, her gaze on the connecting door to the party room as it opened, and Mike reappeared. Tipping his head toward them as he walked across the floor, he said, "Good afternoon, ladies."

Mike went out the front door, and Rachel hurried around the display case of cupcakes and crossed over to the shop's square, six-foot-high, street-side window. She leaned her head toward the glass and watched him take four three-by-three-foot black painted boxes out of the back of a van.

"You should go after him," Andi teased, her voice filled with amusement. "He's very handsome."

"How can you tell?" Rachel drew away from the window, afraid Mike might catch her spying on him. "He's got a black mask covering the upper half of his face. He could have sunken eyes, shaved eyebrows, and facial tattoos."

Andi laughed. "He doesn't, and I know you like guys with dark hair. He's not as tall as my Jake, but he's still got a great build."

"Better not let Jake hear you say that," Rachel retorted. "And how do you know he has a great build? The guy's wrapped in a cape."

"I've seen him before," Andi said. "Without the cape."

"Where?"

"His photo was in the newspaper two weeks ago," Andi confided. "The senior editor at the *Astoria Sun* assigned Jake to write an article on Mike Palmer's set models."

"What are you talking about?"

"Mike Palmer created the miniature model replica of the medieval city of Hilltop for the movie *Battle for Warrior Mountain* and worked on set pieces for many other movies filmed around Astoria. His structural designs are so intricate that when the camera zooms in close, it looks real."

Mike returned through the front door, wheeling in the black boxes on an orange dolly. Rachel caught her breath as he looked her way before proceeding toward the party room with his equipment. Did the masked man find her as intriguing as she found him?

Andi's younger sister, Kim, came in from the kitchen with a large tray of red velvet cupcakes with cherry cream cheese frosting. The three of them together, with Andi's boyfriend, Jake Hartman, as their financial partner, had managed to open Creative Cupcakes a month and a half earlier.

"Who's he?" Kim asked. She placed the cupcakes on the marble counter and pointed toward the billowing black cape of the magician.

"Mike the Magnificent," Rachel said dreamily.

OFFICER IAN LOCKWELL, his wife, son, and daughter entered the shop a short while later. The first time Rachel had met him, he'd written her a parking ticket. Since then, he had helped chase off a group of fanatical Zumba dancers who were trying to shut down Creative Cupcakes and had become one of their biggest supporters. Both were good reasons for her to reverse her original harsh feelings toward the blond, burly man.

"Happy Birthday, Caitlin," Rachel greeted his six-year-old daughter. "Ready for the magic show?"

"I hope he pulls a rabbit out of his hat," Caitlin said, her eyes sparkling. "I asked for a rabbit for my birthday."

"She wanted one last month for Easter," Officer Lockwell confided. "But I told her the bunnies were busy delivering eggs."

"There are always more rabbits in April," Andi told Caitlin and winked conspiratorially at her father. "Aren't there?"

Officer Lockwell shifted his gaze to the ceiling.

"Should we go to the party room?" Rachel asked, leading the way.

"Here are two more," Jake Hartman said, ushering his little girl, Taylor, and Andi's daughter, Mia, into the shop. Both six-year-olds attended the same kindergarten class as Caitlin at Astor Elementary.

Andi stepped forward and gave Jake a kiss before he had to head back to work at the newspaper office.

"Is he a real magician, Mom?" Mia asked Andi, hugging her legs as Mike the Magnificent came out to welcome them.

"As real as they get," Andi assured her.

Rachel exchanged a look with Andi above Mia's head and smiled. "I wonder if he needs an assistant."

In the privacy of the kitchen, Andi pulled the pink bandana off Rachel's hair. "That's better. Now primp your curls."

"And don't forget to swing your hips as you serve the cupcakes," Kim added. "Maybe Magic Mike will wave his wand and whisk you under his cape for a kiss."

"I can hope," Rachel said. "I haven't had a date in two weeks."

"Is that a new record?" Andi teased.

"Almost."

"Maybe if you kept one guy around long enough, you wouldn't have to worry about finding a date," Kim said, arching one of her delicate dark eyebrows.

"Oh, no!" Rachel shook her head. "Rule number one: *Never* date the same man three times in a row. First dates are fabulous, second dates fun, but third dates? That's when guys start to think they freaking know you, and the relationship fails. Better to stick with two dates and forget the rest."

"Jake and I continue to have fun," Andi argued.

"That's because you and Jake are made for each other." Rachel picked up the tray of cupcakes they'd decorated to look like white rabbits peeking out from chocolate top hats. "And so far, I haven't met any man who looks at me the way he looks at you. If I *did*," she said, pausing to make sure her friend got the hint, "I'd marry him."

Andi pushed a strand of her long, dark blond hair behind her ear and blushed. "Maybe Mike will be your man."

"Maybe," Rachel conceded and smiled. "But every re-lationship starts with a first date."

WHEN RACHEL ENTERED the room, Mike was in the middle of performing a card trick. She scanned the faces of the two dozen kids sitting at the long, rectangular tables covered with pink partyware and colorful birthday presents. Mike did a good job of holding their attention. They sat in wide-eyed fascination. Not one of them noticed her as she distributed the cupcakes to each place setting.

Next, Mike the Magnificent showed the audience the inside of his empty black top hat. Placing the hat right-side up on one of his black boxes, he waved his wand over the top and quickly flipped the hat upside down again. Rachel smiled as he invited the birthday girl up to the hat. The six-year-old reached her hand in and pulled out a fake toy bunny with big, white floppy ears.

Caitlin looked at Mike, her eyes betraying her disap-pointment, then mumbled, "Thanks."

"Were you hoping for a real rabbit?" Mike asked her.

Caitlin nodded.

"Let's try that again." Mike told Caitlin to put the stuffed bunny back into the hat. Then he turned the hat over and placed it down on the black box again. He waved the wand. This time when he turned the hat over a live rabbit with big, white floppy ears poked its head up over the top of the rim.

Caitlin let out an excited squeal, and Rachel laughed. Mike the Magnificent was good with the kids and a good magician. How did he do it? She stared at the box and the black hat and couldn't tell how he'd been able to make the switch. Dodging a couple of the strings that hung down from the balloons bobbing against the ceiling, she moved closer.

"Just the person I was looking for," Mike said, catching her eye. "Rachel, could you come up here for a moment?"

"Certainly." Rachel gave him a wide smile and moved to his side. "What would you like me to do?"

"Get in the box."

Rachel glanced at the large horizontal black box resting upon two sawhorses in the middle of the room. It looked eerily like a coffin.

"And take off your shoes," he added under his breath.

Rachel stepped out of her pink pumps, and when Mike moved aside the black curtain covering the box, she slid inside.

"How about a pillow?" Mike asked.

"A pillow would be nice," she said.

His large, warm hand cupped the back of her head as he placed the white cushion beneath her, and his gaze locked with hers. "Are you married?"

Rachel's eyes widened. "No."

"Have a steady boyfriend?"

Rachel shook her head.

"Good," Mike said and grinned at the audience. "I won't have to worry about anyone coming after me if something goes wrong."

"What do you mean, 'if something goes wrong'?" she demanded.

He held up a carpenter's saw with a very large, jagged blade, and the kids in the audience giggled with delight.

"He's going to saw her in half!" Mia exclaimed. "I don't think my mommy will like that. How will Rachel help my mom bake cupcakes?"

"Saw me in half?" Rachel gasped and stared up at Mike. How did this trick work? He wasn't really going to come near her with that saw, was he? "I . . . uh . . . have a slight fear of blades. If I get hurt, do you have a girlfriend or wife I can complain to?"

Mike grinned. "No wife. But if you survive, maybe I'll marry you."

The young audience edged forward in anticipation, probably wondering if they'd see blood or hear her scream.

Rachel had done some pretty crazy things in the past to get a date, but this ridiculous stunt had to top them all. "I really am afraid of blades," she said, her voice raised to a high-pitched squeak.

"Don't worry; I've only killed two people in the past," Mike reassured her, then leaned down to whisper in her ear, "Roll to your side and curl up in a ball."

Rachel did as she was told and faced the audience. There was more room in the box than she'd first supposed. Mike made a few quick adjustments, and an inside board slid up against her feet. Then he raised the shark-toothed blade above her and began to saw the outside of the box in two. The box rattled, and the fresh sawdust made her sneeze, making the kids laugh.

"Does it hurt?" Caitlin asked.

"Not yet," Rachel admitted.

"Here we go," Mike announced.

Rachel closed her eyes, and memories of her uncle filled her mind. Distracted, he'd slipped while working a circular saw and cut off three of his fingers. Blood spurt in every direction. She'd been seven and stood by his side when it happened.

Everyone in the room shouted as Mike pulled the black boxes apart. Rachel frowned. She didn't feel any different.

"Rachel, are you alive?" Mia called out.

"Yes, I'm still here."

Jake's daughter, Taylor, pointed. "Her feet are sticking out of the other half of the box."

"How do you know those feet are mine?" Rachel challenged, knowing her bare toes were still curled beneath her.

Jake's daughter, Taylor, pointed. "Her feet are sticking out of the other half of the box."

"How do you know those feet are mine?" Rachel challenged, knowing her bare toes were curled beneath her.

Caitlin laughed. "They are wearing your pink shoes."

Rachel craned her head around to see the other half of the black box several feet away. The two flesh-colored, lifelike feet sticking out of the end wore her pink pumps.

"How 'bout we put Rachel back together?" Mike suggested.

The kids clapped and cheered.

Moving the two boxes back together, Mike motioned for her to slide out of the first wooden compartment.

Then he removed the set of fake feet out of the second compartment and gave her back her pink pumps. When she'd slipped them on, he took her hand and led her in front of the audience.

"She's back together again!" Mia exclaimed.

"Take a bow," Mike told her. "You've earned it"

"I survived." Rachel tilted her head and gave him a questioning look to remind him of his earlier words. But he didn't ask her to marry him.

He didn't even ask her for a date.

Disappointed, Rachel left the party and headed back to the kitchen, where Andi and Kim waited for a progress report.

"Does he like you?" Andi asked.

"Oh, yes," Rachel said and swallowed the knot in the back of her throat. "He called me a 'good sport.'"

Acknowledgments

I'D LIKE TO thank my editor at Avon Books, Lucia Macro, for giving me the opportunity to write this book series. It's been a dream come true.

And I'd like to thank my critique partners Jennifer Conner, DV Berkom, Chris Karlsen, and Wanda DeGolier for their inspiration and support.

About the Author

Darlene Panzera writes sweet, fun-loving romance and is a member of the Romance Writers of America's Greater Seattle and Peninsula chapters. Her career launched when her novella *The Bet* was picked by Avon Books and *New York Times* bestselling author Debbie Macomber to be published within Debbie's own novel, *Family Affair*. Darlene says, "I love writing stories that help inspire people to laugh, value relationships, and pursue their dreams."

Born and raised in New Jersey, Darlene is now a resident of the Pacific Northwest, where she lives with her husband and three children. When not writing she enjoys spending time with her family and her two horses, and loves camping, hiking, photography, and lazy days at the lake.

Join her on Facebook or at www.darlenepanzera.com.

Give in to your impulses . . .
Read on for a sneak peek at five brand-new
e-book original tales of romance
from Avon Books.
Available now wherever e-books are sold.

STEALING HOME
A DIAMONDS AND DUGOUTS NOVEL
By Jennifer Seasons

LUCKY LIKE US
BOOK TWO: THE HUNTED SERIES
By Jennifer Ryan

STUCK ON YOU
By Cheryl Harper

THE RIGHT BRIDE
BOOK THREE: THE HUNTED SERIES
By Jennifer Ryan

LACHLAN'S BRIDE
HIGHLAND LAIRDS TRILOGY
By Kathleen Harrington

An Excerpt from

STEALING HOME

A DIAMONDS AND DUGOUTS NOVEL

by Jennifer Seasons

When Lorelei Littleton steals Mark Cutter's good
luck charm, all the pro ball player can think is
how good she looked . . . and how bad she'll pay.
Thrust into a contest of wills, they'll both discover
that while revenge may be a dish best served cold,
when it comes to passion, the hotter the better!

Raising his glass, Mark smiled and said, "To the rodeo. May you ride your bronc well."

Color tinged Lorelei's cheeks as they tapped their glasses. But her eyes remained on his while he took a long pull of smooth aged whiskey.

Then she spoke, her voice low. "I'll make your head spin, cowboy. That I promise."

That surprised a laugh out of him, even as heat began to pool heavy in his groin. "I'll drink to that." And he did. He lifted the glass and drained it, suddenly anxious to get on to the next stage. A drop of liquid shimmered on her full bottom lip, and it beckoned him, Reaching an arm out, Mark pulled her close and leaned down. With his eyes on hers, he slowly licked the drop off, his tongue teasing her pouty mouth until she released a soft moan.

Arousal coursed through him at the provocative sound.

Pulling her more fully against him, Mark deepened the kiss. Her lush little body fit perfectly against him, and her lips melted under the heat of his. He slid a hand up her back and fisted the dark, thick mass of her long hair. He loved the feel of the cool, silky strands against his skin.

He wanted more.

Tugging gently, Mark encouraged her mouth to open for him. When it did, his tongue slid inside and tasted, explored the exotic flavor of her. Hunger spiked inside him, and he took the kiss deeper. Hotter. She whimpered into his mouth and dug her fingers into his hair, pulled. Her body began pushing against his, restless and searching.

Mark felt like he'd been tossed into an incinerator when he pushed a thigh between her long, shapely legs and discovered the heat there. He groaned and rubbed his thigh against her, feeling her tremble in response.

Suddenly she broke the kiss and pushed out of his arms. Her breathing was ragged, her lips red and swollen from his kiss. Confusion and desire mixed like a heady concoction in his blood, but before he could say anything, she turned and began walking toward the hallway to his bedroom.

At the entrance she stopped and beckoned to him. "Come and get me, catcher."

So she wanted to play, did she? Hell yeah. Games were his life.

Mark toed off his shoes as he yanked his sweater over his head and tossed it on the floor. He began working the button of his fly and strode after her. He was a little unsteady on his feet, but he didn't care. He just wanted to catch her. When he entered his room, he found her by the bed. She'd turned on the bedside lamp, and the light illuminated every gorgeous inch of her curvaceous body.

He started toward her, but she shook her head. "I want you to sit on the bed."

Mark walked to her anyway and gave her a deep, hungry kiss before he sat on the edge of the bed. He wondered what she had in store for him and felt his gut tighten in anticipation. "Are you going to put on a show for me?" *God, it'd be so hot if she did.*

All she said was "mmm hmm." Then she turned her back to him. Mark let his eyes wander over her body and decided her tight, round ass in denim was just about the sexiest thing he'd ever seen.

When his gaze rose back up, he found her smiling over her shoulder at him. "Are you ready for the ride of your life, cowboy?"

Hell yes he was. "Bring it, baby. Show me what you've got."

Her smile grew sultry with unspoken promise as she reached for the hem of her t-shirt. She pulled it up leisurely while she kept eye contact with him. All he could hear was the soft sound of fabric rustling, but it fueled him—this seductively slow striptease she was giving him.

He wanted to see more of her. "Turn around."

As she turned, she continued to pull her shirt up until she was facing him with the yellow cotton dangling loosely from her fingertips. A black, lacy bra barely covered the most voluptuous, gorgeous pair of breasts he'd ever laid eyes on. He couldn't stop staring.

"Do you like what you see?"

Good God, yes. The woman was a goddess. He nodded, a

little harder than he meant to because he almost fell forward. He was starting to tell her how sexy she was when suddenly a full-blown wave of dizziness hit him. He shook his head to clear it. *What the hell?*

"Is everything all right, Mark?"

The room started spinning, and he tried to stand but couldn't. It felt like the world had been tipped sideways and his body was sliding onto the floor. He tried to stand again but fell backward onto the bed instead. He stared up at her as he tried to right himself and couldn't.

Fonda stood there like a siren, dark hair tousled around her head, breasts barely contained—guilt plastered across her stunning face.

Before he fell unconscious on the bed, he knew. Knew it with gut certainty. He tried to tell her, but his mouth wouldn't move. *Son of a bitch.*

Fonda Peters had drugged him.

An Excerpt from

LUCKY LIKE US

Book Two: The Hunted Series

by Jennifer Ryan

The second installment in The Hunted Series
by Jennifer Ryan . . .

1

A wisp of smoke rose from the barrel of his gun. The smell of gunpowder filled the air. Face raised to the night sky, eyes closed, he sucked in a deep breath and let it out slowly, enjoying the moment. Adrenaline coursed through his veins with a thrill that left a tingle in his skin. His heart pounded, and he felt more alive than he remembered feeling ever in his normal life.

Slowly, he lowered his head to the bloody body lying sprawled on the dirty pavement at his feet. The Silver Fox strikes again. The smile spread across his face. He loved the nickname the press had given him after the police spoke of the elusive killer who'd caused at least eight deaths—who knew how many more? He did. He remembered every one of them in minute detail.

He kicked the dead guy in the ribs. Sonofabitch almost ruined everything, but you didn't get to be in his position by leaving the details in a partnership to chance. They'd had a deal, but the idiot had gotten greedy, making him sloppy. He'd set up a meeting for tonight with a new hit but hadn't done the proper background investigation. His death was a direct result of his stupidity.

"You set me up with a cop!" he yelled at the corpse.

He dragged the body by the foot into the steel container, heedless of the man's face scraping across the rough road. He dropped the guy's leg. The loud thud echoed through the cavernous interior. He locked the door and walked through the deserted shipyard, indifferent.

Maybe he'd let his fury get the best of him, but anything, or anyone, who threatened to expose him or end his most enjoyable hobby needed to be eliminated. He had too much to lose, and he never lost.

Only one more loose end to tie up.

2

San Francisco
Thursday, 9:11 p.m.

Little devils stomped up Sam's spine, telling him trouble was on the way. He rolled his shoulders to erase the eerie feeling, but it didn't work, never did. He sensed something was wrong, and he'd learned to trust his instincts. They'd saved his hide more than once.

Sam and his FBI partner, Special Agent Tyler Reed, sat

in their dark car watching the entrance to Ray's Rock House. Every time someone opened the front door, the blare of music poured out into the otherwise quiet street. Sam's contact hadn't arrived yet, but that was what happened when you relied on the less reputable members of society.

"I've got a weird vibe about this," Sam said, breaking the silence. "Watch the front and alley entrances after I go in."

Tyler never took his eyes off the door and the people coming and going. "I've got your back, but I still think we need more agents on this. What's with you lately? Ever since your brother got married and had a family, you've been on edge, taking one dangerous case after another."

Sam remembered the way his brother looked at his wife and the jealousy that had bubbled up in his gut, taking him by surprise. Jenna was everything to Jack, and since they were identical twins, it was easy for Sam to put himself in Jack's shoes. All he had to do was look at Jack, Jenna, and their two boys to see what it would be like if he found someone to share his life.

Sam had helped Jenna get rid of her abusive ex-husband, who'd kidnapped her a couple years before. Until Jack had come into her life, she'd been alone, hiding from her ex—simply existing, she'd said. Very much like him.

An Excerpt from

STUCK ON YOU

by Cheryl Harper

Love's in the limelight when big-shot producer
KT Masters accidentally picks a fight with
Laura Charles, a single mother working as
a showgirl waitress in a hotel bar. When he
offers her the fling of a lifetime, Laura's willing
to play along . . . just so long as her heart
stays out of it. If she can help it, that is!

Laura said, "Excuse me, Mr. Masters." When he held up an impatient hand, she narrowed her eyes and turned back to the two women. "Maybe you can tell him the drinks are here? I've got other customers to take care of."

The pink-haired woman held out a hand. "Sure thing. I'm Mandy, the makeup artist. This is Shane. She'll do hair. We'll both help with costumes and props as needed."

As Laura shook their hands, she privately thought that might be the best arrangement. Shane's hair was perfect, not one strand out of place. Mandy's pink shag sort of made it look like she'd been caught in a windstorm. In a convertible. But her makeup and clothes were very cute.

KT said, "Hold on just a sec, Bob. Let me go ahead and tweet this. Gotta keep the fans interested, you know."

Laura glanced over her bare shoulder to see KT bound down the stairs, pause, snap a picture, and then type something on his phone before shouting about taking down the electronic display in the corner. Lucky would not be happy about that. As KT waved his arms dramatically and the director nodded, Laura smiled at the two girls. "Guess I'm dismissed."

They laughed, and Laura turned to skirt their table as she reached for the drink tray. Being unable to move, like her feathers had attached themselves to the floor, was her first clue that something had gone horribly wrong. And when KT Masters bumped into her, sending the tray skidding into the sodas she'd just delivered, she knew exactly who was responsible. She tried to whirl around to give him a piece of her mind but spun in place and then heard a loud rip just before she bumped into the table and sent two glasses crashing to the floor. She might have followed them, but KT wrapped a hand around her arm to steady her. His warm skin was a brand against her chilly flesh.

The only sound in Viva Las Vegas was the tinny *plink* of electricity through one million bright white bulbs. Every eye was focused on the drama taking place at the foot of the stage. Before she could really get a firm grip on the embarrassment, irritation, shock, and downright anger boiling over, Laura shouted, "You ripped off my feather!"

Even the light bulbs seemed to hold their breath at that point.

KT's hand slid down her arm, raising goose bumps as it went, before he slammed both hands on his hips, and Laura shivered. The heat from that one hand made her wonder what it would be like to be pressed up against him. Instead of the flannel robe, she should put a KT Masters on her birthday list. She wouldn't have to worry about being cold ever again.

"Yeah, I did you a favor. This costume has real potential"—he motioned with one hand as he looked her over from collarbone to knee—"but the feathers get in the way, so . . . you're welcome!" The frown looked all wrong on his face, like he didn't have a lot of experience with anger or irritation, but the look in his eyes was as warm as his hand had been. When he rubbed his palms together, she thought maybe she wasn't the only one to be surprised by the heat.

They both looked down at the bedraggled pink feather, now swimming in ice cubes and spilled soda under his left shoe. No matter how much she hated the feathers or how valid his point about their ridiculousness was, she wasn't going to let him get away with this. He should apologize. Any decent person would.

"What are you going to do about it?" She plopped her hands on her own hips, thrust her chin out, and met his angry stare.

He straightened and flashed a grim smile before leaning down to scrape the feather up off the floor. He pinched the driest edge and held it out from his body. "Never heard 'the customer's always right,' have you?"

Laura snatched the feather away. "In what way are you a customer? I only see a too-important big shot who can't apologize."

His opened his mouth to say . . . something, then changed his mind and pointed a finger in her face instead. "Oh, really? I bet if I went to have a little talk with the manager or Miss

Willodean, they'd have a completely different take on what just happened here and who needs to apologize."

Laura narrowed her eyes and tilted her head. "Oh, really? I'll take that bet."

An Excerpt from

THE RIGHT BRIDE
Book Three: The Hunted Series

by Jennifer Ryan

The Hunted Series continues with this
third installment by Jennifer Ryan . . .

1

Shelly swiped the lip gloss wand across her lips, rolled them in and out to smooth out the color, and grinned at herself in the mirror, satisfied with the results. She pushed up her boobs, exposing just enough flesh to draw a man's attention, and keep it, but still not look too obvious.

"Perfect. He'll love it."

Ah, Cameron Shaw. Rich and powerful, sexy as hell, and kind in a way that made it easy to get what she wanted. Exactly the kind of husband she'd always dreamed about marrying.

Shelly had grown up in a nice middle class family. Ordinary. She desperately wanted to be anything but ordinary.

She'd grown up a plump youngster and a fat teenager. At fifteen, she'd resorted to binging and purging and starved herself thin. Skinny and beautiful—boys took notice. You can get a guy to do just about anything when you offer them hot sex. By the time she graduated high school, she'd transformed herself into the most popular girl in the place.

For Shelly, destined to live a glamorous life in a big house with servants and fancy cars and clothes, meeting Cameron in the restaurant had been a coup.

Executives and wealthy businessmen frequented the upscale restaurant. She'd gone fishing and landed her perfect catch. Now, she needed to hold on and reel in a marriage proposal.

2

Night fell outside Cameron's thirty-sixth-floor office window. Tired, he'd spent all day in meetings. For the president of Merrick International, long hours were the norm and sleepless nights were a frequent occurrence.

The sky darkened and beckoned the stars to come to life. If he were out on the water, and away from the glow of the city lights, he'd see them better, twinkling in all their brilliant glory.

He couldn't remember the last time he'd taken out the sailboat. He'd promised Emma he'd take her fishing. Every time he planned to go, something came up at work. More and more often, he put her off in favor of some deal or problem that couldn't wait. He needed to realign his priorities. His daughter deserved better.

He stared at the picture of his golden girl. Emma was five now and the image of her mother: long, wavy golden hair and deep blue eyes. She always looked at him with such love. He remembered Caroline looking at him the same way.

They'd been so happy when they discovered Caroline was pregnant. In the beginning, things had been so sweet. They'd lain awake at night talking about whether it would be a boy or a girl, what they'd name their child, and what they thought he or she would grow up to be.

He never thought he'd watch his daughter grow up without Caroline beside him.

The pregnancy took a turn in the sixth month when Caroline began having contractions. They gave her medication to stop them and put her on bed rest for the rest of the pregnancy.

One night he'd come home to find her pale and hurting. He rushed her to the hospital. Her blood pressure spiked, and the contractions started again. No amount of medication could stop them. Two hours later, when the contractions were really bad, the doctor came in to tell him Caroline's body was failing. Her liver and kidneys were shutting down.

Caroline was a wreck. He still heard her pleading for him to save the baby. She delivered their daughter six weeks early, then suffered a massive stroke and died without ever holding her child.

Cameron picked up the photograph and traced his daughter's face, the past haunting his thoughts. He'd spent three weeks in the Neonatal Intensive Care Unit, grieving for his wife and begging his daughter to live. Week four had been a turning point. He felt she'd spent three weeks mourning the loss of her mother and then decided to live for her father. She began eating on her own and gained weight quickly. Ten days later, Cameron finally took his daughter home. From then on, it had been the two of them.

Almost a year ago, he'd decided enough was enough. Emma needed a mother.

An Excerpt from

LACHLAN'S BRIDE
HIGHLAND LAIRDS TRILOGY
by Kathleen Harrington

Lady Francine Walsingham can't believe
Lachlan MacRath, laird and pirate, is to be her
escort into Scotland. But trust him she must, for
Francine has no choice but to act as his lover to
keep her enemies at bay. When Lachlan first sees
Francine, the English beauty stirs his blood like
no woman has ever before. And now that they
must play the besotted couple so he can protect
her, Lachlan is determined to use all his seductive
prowess to properly woo her into his bed.

May 1496
The Cheviot Hills
The Border Between England and Scotland

Stretched flat on the blood-soaked ground, Lachlan Mac-Rath gazed up at the cloudless morning sky and listened to the exhausted moans of the wounded.

The dead and the dying lay scattered across the lush spring grass. Overhead, the faint rays of dawn broke above the hilltops as the buttercups and bluebells dipped and swayed in the soft breeze. The gruesome corpses were sprawled amidst the wildflowers, their vacant eyes staring upward to the heavens, the stumps of their severed arms and legs still oozing blood and gore. Dented helmets, broken swords, axes, and pikes gave mute testimony to the ferocity of the combatants. Here and there, a loyal destrier, trained to war, grazed calmly alongside its fallen master.

Following close upon daylight, the scavengers would come

creeping, ready to strip the bodies of anything worth a shilling: armor, dirks, boots, belts. If they were Scotsmen, he'd be in luck. If not, he'd soon be dead. There wasn't a blessed thing he could do but wait. He was pinned beneath his dead horse, and all efforts to free himself during the night had proven fruitless.

In the fierce battle of the evening before, the warriors on horseback had left behind all who'd fallen. Galloping across the open, rolling countryside, Scots and English had fought savagely, until it was too dark to tell friend from foe. There was no way of knowing the outcome of the battle, for victory had been determined miles away.

Hell, it was Lachlan's own damn fault. He'd come on the foray into England with King James for a lark. After delivering four new cannons to the castle at Roxburgh, along with the Flemish master gunners to fire them, he'd decided not to return to his ship immediately as planned. The uneventful crossing on the *Sea Hawk* from the Low Countries to Edinburgh, followed by the tedious journey to the fortress, with the big guns pulled by teams of oxen, had left him eager for a bit of adventure.

When he'd learned that the king was leading a small force into Northumberland to retrieve cattle raided by Sassenach outlaws, the temptation to join them had been too great to resist. There was nothing like a hand-to-hand skirmish with his ancient foe to get a man's blood pumping through his veins.

But Lord Dacre, Warden of the Marches, had surprised the Scots with a much larger, well-armed force of his own, and what should have been a carefree rout had turned into deadly combat.

A plea for help interrupted Lachlan's brooding thoughts.

Not far away, a wounded English soldier who'd cried out in pain during the night raised himself up on one elbow.

"Lychester! Over here, sir! It's Will Jeffries!"

Lachlan watched from beneath slit lids as another Sassenach came into view. Attired in the splendid armor of the nobility, the newcomer rode a large, caparisoned black horse. He'd clearly come looking for someone, for he held the reins of a smaller chestnut, its saddle empty and waiting.

"Here I am, Marquess," the young man named Jeffries called weakly. He lifted one hand in a trembling wave as the Marquess of Lychester drew near to his countryman. Dismounting, he approached the wounded soldier.

"Thank God," Jeffries said with a hoarse groan. "I've taken a sword blade in my thigh. The cut's been oozing steadily. I was afraid I wouldn't make it through the night."

Lychester didn't say a word. He came to stand behind the injured man, knelt down on one knee, and raised his fallen comrade to a seated position. Grabbing a hank of the man's yellow hair, the marquess jerked the fair head back and deftly slashed the exposed throat from ear to ear. Then he calmly wiped his blade on the youth's doublet, lifted him up in his arms, and threw the body facedown over the chestnut's back.

The English nobleman glanced around, checking, no doubt, to see if there'd been a witness to the coldblooded execution. Lachlan held his breath and remained motionless, his lids still lowered over his eyes. Apparently satisfied, the marquess mounted, grabbed the reins of the second horse, and rode away.

Lachlan slowly exhaled.

Sonofabitch.